price ·less

ˈprīsləs/

adjective

1. so precious that its value cannot be
determined.
"priceless works of art"

○ *informal*
used to express great and usually affectionate
amusement.
"darling, you're priceless!"

Priceless

The ROTHVALE LEGACY

I

RAINE MILLER

Copyright © 2014 *Raine Miller Romance*
All rights reserved.
Cover: *Mae I Design Photography*
Editing: *Making Manuscripts*

ISBN: 1942095007
ISBN-13: 978-1942095002

Raine Miller Romance

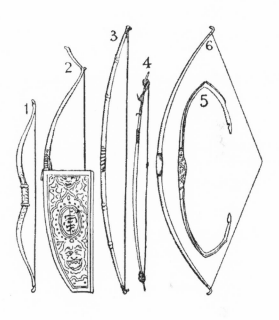

DEDICATION

For Amanda

I saw the angel in the marble and carved until I set *her* free...

—Michelangelo (1475 - 1564)

CONTENTS

ACKNOWLEDGMENTS

I began to write this story over two years ago. It was envisioned and outlined before I ever penned *Naked*. Yes, it's true. I have my composition book with the original notes to prove it. It's all there in black and white. I treasure that simple book with the handwritten ideas and scribblings about a reluctant Lord of the Realm and a stubborn art conservationist. Of course, it all got put on hold when I found my inspiration for Ethan Blackstone and Brynne Bennett's story in the Blackstone Affair ... but I never forgot about my original characters of Gaby and Ivan. In fact, I placed them smack dab in the middle of my Blackstone world on purpose so I <u>couldn't</u> forget about them. I wrote their beginnings into the climax at the end of ***All In*** so that I'd be forced to tell their story at some point. A very small portion of ***Priceless***, mostly just the beginning, was published in the ***Stories for Amanda*** anthology to raise support for the *Amanda Todd Foundation* and awareness against bullying. I am happy to be bringing the full story to you now. I've fielded questions from loyal readers for the past two years asking patiently when might they get to finally know what was going on with our Ivan and Gaby all this time. Well, you're about to find out, so a huge THANK YOU to my persistent fans. This one is all because of YOU.

xxoo R

Chapter 1

London
29ᵗʰ June

C harity galas.

Bloody *horrific* if you ask me, and a perfectly accurate descriptor for them. Since I was about to give up my evening for one, I could call it whatever I liked.

The annual Mallerton Society bunfight would surely be no different, so I imagined surviving the next couple of hours would be mission number one for me. Well, I did have a little entertainment to look forward to near the end of the evening and that was about the only redeeming part.

I pulled into the National Gallery, queued for

valet service, and checked my mobile for the details.

There it was. I read it twice and attempted to memorize who, what, and where. **Maria will be wearing an emerald green gown. Victorian Gallery 9:00 p.m. Terms per contract. We wish you both a very pleasant evening.**

The escort service I used was one that didn't have a name and you never talked to anyone by voice. Everything was transacted by text. Simple. Efficient. Anonymous. No strings attached to get all tangled into a cocked-up mess, and when the date was over everyone went home satisfied.

The less time I had to think about what I was really doing, the better. I wasn't proud of my behavior, but the reasons were justified in my mind. I was just exploiting what was offered in order to get by.

Betrayal does that to a man.

By the time I made my way inside and found the venue, I was pleasantly surprised to see I'd missed the dinner. The polite conversation required at these kind of events was sheer torture for me, and I often wondered how on earth that I, out of all of the eligible men in England, could have ended up inheriting a directorship on the board of The Gallery. There couldn't possibly be a worse choice *than* me. I knew next to nothing about paintings, and possessed no inclination to begin learning about them, either. Being Lord Rothvale in the twenty-first century was a pretentious millstone around my neck. Having patrons address me as "my Lord" and bowing upon introduction made my skin crawl.

I was left having to fake it.

I did that a lot.

The pretense grew very tiresome to me because my whole life had been turned upside down by lies. Hung, drawn and quartered by the media. Yeah, pretty much. At least, it sure felt like it at the time. Now I was rather more numb than anything. My Bombay Sapphire worked wonders.

False…counterfeit…sham.

Where in the bloody hell had they set the bar up in this place?

I wandered a bit, trying to appear focused on the exhibit and praying nobody recognized me for fifteen minutes. Hell, I'd be happy with five, if I could grab even that.

The landscape changed for a pleasant turn when I spotted the lovely Brynne Bennett presenting a painting of a woman with a book. It looked like it could be a Mallerton in the midst of the conservation process. It was being repaired or preserved so it could last another hundred years or so without losing its colours and clarity of image. Yes, I'd managed to absorb a few bits of knowledge about what needed to happen to old paintings by default. I'd much rather enjoy the view of the stunning conservator giving the presentation of the art, though.

Brynne was very easy to look at, but she was also very taken. By none other than my obsessively protective cousin. Ethan runs a security business so I give him credit for the *protective* part. He has excellent taste in women. I give him that, too.

"Enjoying the show?" I wasn't surprised when Ethan's voice came from behind at my shoulder. I should have known he'd be within striking distance of his beloved.

"Probably more like wondering when in the hell I might be able to *escape* the show," I answered. "I was just thinking about you, cousin."

"Really." he drawled.

"Indeed. Think of the devil and he appears as if by magic."

"Glad you could make it tonight," he said sarcastically. "We've been wondering when you'd finally grace us with your presence. Brynne wants to introduce you to her friend." He looked around as if he were searching the crowd for someone.

"Brynne looks very busy right now." I glanced over at his girlfriend admiringly. "Maybe later, I need a drink."

Ethan's jaw hardened. "Look, Ivan, there was a pseudo threat delivered to my office today. I'm not horribly concerned but I want you frontloaded on the details." He handed me an envelope of photos.

Ethan and I had done this plenty of times before so it wasn't anything new. Eight-by-ten black and white photographs of Brynne and me chatting at Gladstone's, where I'd met the two of them for lunch a few weeks back. Me kissing her on the cheeks, as I put her in the car. Me leaning in to speak to the both of them, and waving them off. Me on the street after Ethan had pulled the car away. Me waiting on the street for my own car to come 'round from valet.

I grunted at the photos as I ran through them a second time, flipping over the pictures one by one.

Nothing written.

Until the last one: *"Never attempt to murder a man who is committing suicide"* scrawled on the back.

Marvelous. Another fan sending me love notes. I'd forgotten how fucked in the head some of them were. Here was my reminder.

I'd seen this kind of thing throughout my career. It had to be taken seriously of course, but more often than not, it was some lunatic fringe who had an axe to grind on the back of a notable they perceived to have caused offense to them personally, and with cruel intent. Sports figures especially suffered this kind of crap. I had offended a ton of people in my time and had the gold medals to prove it. Even though I was retired from the sport, I was still hounded by the media continually. The hounding had grown especially fierce with what had recently happened in my private life. The upcoming Olympic Games being hosted in my home country didn't help either. It put me back on the radar and the timing couldn't have been worse. I'd be commentating men's archery for the BBC in less than a month.

"Another super fan come to pay his respects," I said dismissively. The real truth was I counted my blessings having Ethan as blood family. That alone would have earned his protection regardless, but I certainly kept him busy. After a minute, I handed the whole lot of ridiculousness back to him as if it didn't matter. The honest part of me knew it didn't really. I was past the point of getting worked up over tedious shit, and far too used to this brand of attention to get really upset. I was realistic enough to know this wouldn't be the last time I received a threat. They arrived as regular as estate taxes. "Thanks, E, for looking out. I'm sure it'll all flag off when the Olympics are but a memory."

He nodded slowly, his jaw tight as he glanced over at his girl once more who was skillfully presenting conservation technique to a rapt audience.

I looked at the drink in his hand and decided that getting one for myself was a bigger priority now than it had been earlier. And two G & T's was a far more accurate estimate than just the one if I wanted to feel even a little better.

"At least I can hope, true?" I acted like I didn't care about the threat.

"It's all any of us can do, mate." E clapped me on the back with one hand.

"I need to have something along the lines of what you're having." I waved off and left for the bar, in a worse mood than I'd been a few moments ago.

If that was even possible.

WEARING a new dress is always fun, and I loved how this one felt against my skin. Halter neck with a floaty skirt. Brynne's Aunt Marie had taken us both to a fabulous shop in Knightsbridge that sold vintage gowns. The emerald floral silk moved so well as I walked, I couldn't help but be impressed with the superior artistry. It definitely paid to buy quality. I'd bought the gown specifically for tonight's occasion and figured it was wise to invest in something I could wear to other formal events I'd be required to attend through the university. And the party was as beautiful as ever. *The Annual Mallerton Society Gala for the Arts* in honor of Romanticist painter, Sir Tristan Mallerton, was something I'd attended four years running. I knew his birthday as well as I knew the birthdays of my own family. June 29th. I ought to know. His work was the basis for my Master's in Art History at University of London. Inspiration in the form of a painting handed down through the generations of my family, and that I had loved my whole life. It was a minor work of Mallerton's, but it would belong to me one day, and had sparked the seed of interest for my studies and hopefully my life's work.

I knew every catalogued painting Mallerton had done, and had seen a good portion of them. The National Gallery had custody of the largest collection of his work on display in Britain, but it was a safe bet there were plenty of unknowns in private homes and in storage that had never seen the light of day. Mallerton had been a prolific painter during his lifetime. Most of those pieces were in the hands of people who had no idea what they owned, and sadly, no interest in finding out either. Occasionally, a painting would come onto the market from a private collection and go to auction though. And it was my job to have it evaluated and entered into the database.

I stopped at an equestrian portrait that I counted among my top five favorites out of all of his work. It was a happy painting, and every time I saw it I wanted to smile. Mallerton had executed it perfectly, the moment preserved in time for all to enjoy.

The subject was a young bride with long dark hair seated on a magnificent pale horse adorned with garlands and ribbons and bells throughout his tack. Even though she wasn't smiling at all like a person would today when posing for a picture, the expression of joy captured so exquisitely in her expression made you a believer. There was no doubt this girl was a happy bride. It was titled simply, *Mrs. Gravelle*, and always made me wonder what Mr. Gravelle was like. He'd won a beautiful bride that's for sure, and I dearly hoped he'd loved her as he should have.

Even the most unsophisticated observer could see the emotion in Mallerton's work. The ability to make people emote is a true artistic gift. Tristan Mallerton was blessed with that ability without a doubt. It was the thing that'd drawn me to his work in particular when I'd begun my studies. Plus the fact my father owned an original Mallerton portrait.

Passed down through the years of Hargreave descendants, it was of Sophie Hargreave, my great, great, great, grandmother, and would someday be mine.

I loved the formal pose of her in a gorgeous blue and white gown, her incredibly long mahogany hair artfully arranged to the side, but it was her expression that ruled the portrait. There was an air of amusement to her smile. The elegant Sophie possessed a mischievous twinkle in her pretty eyes, suggesting she wasn't all seriousness and convention.

And Mallerton's rare talent of portraying the subjects of his paintings in such a way that had you wondering about who the people were, and their life's story, just made the portrait all the more interesting. Something for which Mallerton was known. Quite simply, his art left you craving for more. Who were the people in his portraits? Whom did they love? Why was a particular pose or setting chosen for the subject? These very questions, still asked today, were the exact essence of Mallerton's talent, which had given him such acclaim, both in his lifetime, and now, two hundred four years later.

Two hundred years. Four years. They might as well be the same thing. A lot could change in just four years…

You've changed.

I tried not to think about what I'd lost, but my self-imposed loneliness got the better of me sometimes, and I'd be lying if I couldn't admit I longed for even a portion of the bliss Mrs. Gravelle had in her painting.

The chances of you ever finding someone who will inspire you to look like the bride in that painting is slim to none—

"I found you," a smooth voice said behind me.

I turned to see who was speaking to me and got an eyeful of beautiful. The man before me was six feet plus of dark, lean and sexy with green eyes the color of my dress. He flashed me a smile that could only be described as wicked.

"Are you sure you were looking for me?" He appeared to have money because I'd bet my extravagant new gown the tux hanging off his fine form was most certainly bespoke. No doubt about it. Was he a patron in need of a gallery tour? A large contributor VIP?

"Oh yes, it's definitely you," he purred, "the beauty in the green dress." He leaned forward. Close but not touching, his face tilted toward my neck. I backed up. He followed...until I was pressed against the wall. "And they were so right," he said in his silky voice.

"Right about what?" I asked, mesmerized by his features and his delicious scent, and totally overpowered by how close he was to me. My God, he smelled good. "Um…d-did you want a t-tour?" I stuttered, amazed coherent words were even forming from my lips.

"Mmm hmm," he said, nodding slowly, drawing his gaze up my neck, "I definitely want *your* tour."

Why are you speaking like that to me? I was clearly at a disadvantage in this situation and could definitely feel the weirdness coming at me from all directions.

Who was this Greek god trapping me against the wall, looking like he wanted to devour me? And was it bad that the thought of him actually doing some devouring made a long shiver roll down my back?

Mr. Man-Beauty didn't appear to be in any hurry, his green eyes tracking over my body, roving over everything they could see.

I swallowed hard.

"Who—who was it that sent you to find me, ah…mister—?"

"—Ivanhoe. The service notified you, right?" He inhaled and moved a fraction closer, just staring with a confident half-smirk on his face. "You're definitely who I'm supposed to meet tonight. Nine o'clock and wearing a green dress, which by the way is very…*very*…nice." The last three words were spoken slowly as his eyes raked up my dress until he landed somewhere around my lips.

"Nine o'clock," I repeated dumbly, overwhelmed by his maleness and his friggin' gorgeous…everything, to the point I had apparently lost the ability to carry on a conversation.

Wait. Service?

"So you are Mr. Ivanhoe, and you want me to give you the tour." I said a tad too sarcastically, wanting to slap myself for the ignorance that kept spouting out of my mouth.

I was in utter and complete bewilderment of what was going on with him though.

I *knew* for a fact I hadn't been informed about any VIP named Mr. Ivanhoe needing a contributor's tour tonight during the gala. But it was clearly what he was expecting, standing boldly, looking like a man who was *very* sure of what he wanted. I couldn't just say no and blow him off. It would be incredibly rude and possibly get me into trouble with the university. And that was the thing with VIPs. They tended to be less predictable and often showed up, expecting special treatment. Their deep pockets were what kept the charities going though, and offending a generous donor was a big no-no.

He tilted his head and narrowed his eyes a little, his brow wrinkling for an instant. "Call me that if you wish, I don't mind, and yes, I want whatever you have arranged for me." He brushed back his hair with a hand and held it there gripping at the back of his neck, his elbow coming up and framing me in even more. "I'm ready to begin if you are." He smiled.

Whatever I have arranged? I had nothing planned. I had no idea why any of this conversation between us was even happening. I knew nothing. Well, I knew one thing—I couldn't take my eyes off his hair.

Mr. Ivanhoe's hair was dark and straight, worn deliciously long in the European style, hitting just above where his broad shoulders met his neck. I wanted to touch.

He'd been blessed in more ways than just his wallet. *An alien perhaps?*

"All right," I said carefully, swallowing hard again, and wondering just how the next thirty minutes were going to go with the each of us staring and speaking in some kind of mysterious code. "Where would you like to start, Mr. Ivanhoe? What are your main interests?"

He offered his arm, which I accepted and let him lead us into the hallway.

"Beauty interests me right now." He looked down at me and smiled darkly, his lips slightly parted and my arm tucked firmly under his.

It interests me, too. "Well, there is plenty of beauty here to show you," I said.

"I thought so." He stopped us at a door. "I can't wait to see it all and experience it for myself."

He opened the door and led me inside a darkened anteroom. Various works in progress of restoration and archival rooms were down this way. I was about to ask him if he wanted a tour of the conservationist wing when he shut the door and pressed me back against it. "Bloody perfect," he mumbled.

"What—?" was all I managed to get out before he took my face in his hands, slammed his mouth down over mine, and started kissing me with his beautiful mouth.

MY "date" was interesting tonight. Sexy as all get-out but mysteriously illusive with what sounded to be a Yank accent. And so damn beautiful my eyes were stinging.

We really needed to get this party started, and we couldn't very well just stand here in a quiet gallery hallway mentally undressing each other now, could we? It would be wholly inappropriate, and someone was bound to come by and see eventually.

I don't usually go in for public shags but was far too gone in attraction to my "tour guide" to care very much. I'm a man of action. Give me a problem and I will do my bloody best to find a solution.

Like right now for instance: *Where can I find a place to get Maria alone and see what she's got hidden beneath her sexy gown?*

Was Maria really her name? I tried to remember the text I'd received, and thought I was right, but details like that slip my mind consistently. I *was* however, well aware how escorts didn't like for clients to use their working names where somebody might hear.

I always followed the rules with the ladies, still shocked this beautiful creature was an escort in the first place and not a model for Vogue or Harpers. She could be, in a heartbeat.

A door appeared in front of me, so I opened it and brought her in with me. Dark, empty, private. "Bloody perfect," I said.

I pressed her up against the door and took her face in my hands. Her eyes were a stunning dark green, almost the same colour as mine were, but I just had to get to know that luscious mouth of hers first.

I could look into her eyes once we were shagging in a few, and I planned on it.

I wanted a taste of those lips mostly, and then I'd move on to other parts. I knew what I was doing and I was totally confident she did, as well.

"What—?" she murmured, just as I descended.

The time for talking has well passed, lovely thing.

When I covered her mouth with mine and got a first taste, something switched on inside me and I sort of lost my normally maintained control.

I just wanted to push my way in and get lost in her for a while.

She froze at first and sucked in a breath, but then she seemed to soften and give way, and started to kiss me back. She tasted like a delicious wine I couldn't seem to get enough of, so I just delved deeper and held her firmly.

It took a moment, but I felt her response grow to the point where her hands got into the action and buried in my hair. Once that started happening I knew everything was good. We had chemistry together and I was sure of one thing—I'd be getting Maria's number so we could do this again.

I moved a hand down to sweep under her skirt and slid my palm up her thigh and right between her legs. I felt lace.

And a bundle of hot, sexy female.

"Ahhh…" she moaned, standing up on her toes and throwing her head back when I touched her. I moved my mouth to her throat and down the deep neckline of her dress. My fingers dove under the lace of her knickers and found my target, skimming back and forth where it counted.

That she was totally turned on and primed for action, was never in question. I had the proof over my fingers.

This goddess in my arms, wearing a green dress I wished I could strip her out of, was about to come on me. *Fucking hot.*

I gripped her face with my free hand and brought her back to face me. "Open your eyes."

She complied instantly, her lashes flipping up and revealing those green beauties I'd admired earlier. Her breathing was coming in heavy pants now. Time to hit a bullseye with Miss Maria, I decided.

I moved two fingers into position and buried them inside her. In the same moment I seized her mouth and impaled myself there, too. She was totally mine to conquer and I relished the control in moments like this. I was all about control when it came to sex.

Especially now.

I matched the stroking of my fingers with the pace of my tongue, and in no time, I had her riding the wave of an orgasm as she rode my hand.

I swallowed her tensing cries with my mouth, and slowed everything down for her until she was completely melted against the door, fighting for breaths.

Mission accomplished.

"God, you're beautiful." She widened her eyes and focused on me, a look of utter satisfaction simmering in them as she breathed against the door. What I wouldn't give to have her in my bed right now. The possibilities flashed in images through my head as I moved my fingers slowly out, retreating carefully from her body. She gasped softly and rolled with my movements, coming down from the rush to stand on her own again. Her head was slightly tilted and resting on the back of the door. My hand still on her face, I lowered it down to her shoulder, caressing as I went.

"My turn," I told her.

Her eyes flared at me in the dim light for an instant, as if she were considering my request, but the afterglow of pleasure boiling in her eyes told me she was *very* into what we were doing. We were just getting started on where I planned for this to go.

She sighed in contentment and dropped down to her knees gracefully before me, her fine hands reaching forward to work on opening my trousers. She pulled out my shirt and found my cock, which was more than ready to meet her pretty mouth. I couldn't hold back the groan that came out of me and closed my eyes in anticipation.

It had been a while and I was definitely going to enjoy this.

When she touched me I thrust into her hand. She gripped the shaft and stroked, pulling me closer. I felt the softness of her tongue slide over the tip of me and welcomed the hot burn of pleasure.

My fantasy lover was just getting into the groove, and doing a superb job I might add, when our timing went to complete shit.

The emergency light above the door began to twirl a flashing red, and was paired with an ear-deafening decibels siren wail. Over all of that, the loudspeaker announcement demanded the building be exited immediately for safety precautions.

Well, damn, this certainly sucked.

Or not.

Maria was off me and out the door before I could get myself tucked back into my trousers.

By the time I managed to stumble out of our little love nest, she was nowhere to be seen, but Ethan was sprinting down the hallway.

I ran for it, coming up behind him. He turned back and saw me.

"Bomb threat. That's what this is." He gestured

to the flashing lights. "Everyone's being evacuated."

I exploded in anger, unbelieving that someone would hate me so much they would blow up a museum to get to me. Disgruntled fan or not, an act of terrorism was way out of bounds. "Are you fucking joking? All this because of me?"

"I don't know details. I was out having a smoke when the alarm went off. Neil said in-house security received a bomb threat and they're closing everything down. We'll sort it later. Just get the fuck out!"

So that's what I did.

I looked for Maria but I never found her in the crush of people swarming the front steps of the National Gallery. I thought I saw her at one point because there was a woman wearing a similar colour green dress, but she was blonde and definitely not the fiery goddess I'd been with in that room earlier.

Pity. I would have asked her home with me and paid double for her services without a second thought. Maria was definitely worth it.

A bottle of Bombay and a session with her would've topped off my evening just perfectly. I texted Ethan to let him know I was leaving and to ring me when he had a chance. As I drove home to my solitary existence, I wasn't content and certainly wasn't satisfied.

I felt like shit and there were plenty of other

reasons for that, unfortunately. The only nice thing to happen tonight had been the encounter with a beautiful creature whose sexy scent was still clinging to my hand.

I brought the back of the fingers I'd used on her up to just under my nose where I could breathe in the unmistakable lingering of female. Lovely...and fucking sexy.

The smell of pussy and my unsatisfied cock was not a good combination though, and it put me into an even darker mood. Damn. Wanking off was not something I envisioned as part of my scheduled evening, but I'd end up doing it tonight. Something had to take my edge off and a certain someone's essence would be a damn fine stimulus to helping matters along.

I was determined to find Maria again, and had no doubts I would, too. We had unfinished business to conduct, and the service owed me a date. I would make sure they knew to send her as soon as it could be arranged.

I wouldn't be able to forget her until I sampled all she had to offer. *Until I have her right where I want and at my mercy, taking my cock.*

I grinned as I turned onto my street in St. James and drove through the gates.

I know myself pretty well. When I want

something, I won't stop until I've conquered the challenge. Right now my challenge was a green-eyed beauty that had, for whatever reason, bewitched me this evening.

Remarkable…

Chapter 2

The floor plan of the National Gallery was something I knew like the back of my hand. A small blessing for which I felt supremely grateful, running as fast as my heels would carry me. I didn't allow my mind to dwell on what I'd just done with a complete stranger. I fled. Get away first, figure out my horrifying lapse in judgment later.

Pray he doesn't see you. Pray, Gabrielle. Pray very hard.

Security directed everyone out of the National Gallery with the command, *"Evacuate the building without delay!"* on constant repeat over the loudspeaker. I overheard the words "bomb threat" more than once, too. But none of that deterred me from my goal. I had to get out of here.

I didn't even look through the crowds of people milling about on the steps to see if I could spot Brynne and Ethan. I knew Ethan would get my roommate out safely, and whatever was going on with the security of the paintings and the gallery itself was far beyond my control.

Just get away for now...

I saw Neil McManus, Ethan's executive partner at Blackstone Security, and waved to let him know I was on my way out of the building so he could relay it to anyone who might wonder about me. I was getting the hell out of here and waiting around for a roll call wasn't happening. I might see *him* again. Mr. Ivanhoe. I'd die if I had to face that man again right now. Just collapse and die right here on the steps of the National Gallery.

So I did something I've done before in similar situations.

I ran for safety.

Fleeing down the steps, I made my way up to the corner, hailing the first taxi I could. When a London black cab pulled up to the pavement, I pushed out a big breath of air in sheer relief, realizing I'd been holding it. I slid into the back seat and gave the driver my address, feeling suddenly exhausted. I kept my head down and wished I could disappear as he pulled quickly out into traffic.

"What's all that then?" he asked.

"The fire alarm just went off and they told everyone to get out. I don't know, but I heard the words 'bomb threat' as I passed by a security guard talking into his earpiece."

My driver snorted in disgust, and mumbled something about the country going to "bloody hell," and went back to navigating the streets.

I allowed myself to silently fall apart in the back of his cab, still in shock at what I'd done with a man I didn't even know. What was wrong with me? How could I have permitted him to—touch me like that? To kiss me like that?

If the situation I found myself in wasn't so horrifying I'd be far more concerned about the reason for the evacuation and the safety of the art in the first place. The sad truth was I didn't give the alarm much thought at all beyond the fact it had interrupted something I shouldn't have *ever* been doing. My head was so screwed up right now with thoughts of what'd just happened in a side room with Mr. Ivanhoe I couldn't spare any more of my emotions on worry about the paintings, or otherwise.

Priceless

An orgasm happened, you freak.

What in the bloody hell was he about anyway? Who does that? Goes up to a random woman and seduces her in a closet?

The better question was what woman allows such a thing to happen with zero protest? That would be me. *Slut. You're such a slutty whore, and you have zero self-control, that's why!*

I tried to sort out the sequence of events but none of it made any sense. He'd walked up behind me and said, "I found you," as if he knew I'd be there waiting for him. Mr. Ivanhoe hadn't seemed confused at all, but acted as if our meeting had been planned in advance. He'd even mentioned my green dress. I wondered if Paul Langley had arranged for the VIP tour and forgotten to tell me. But that didn't make any sense either because Mr. Ivanhoe was not about getting a tour of the museum. He'd been all about getting a blow job from me. *And you had his cock in your mouth, and were giving him one when the alarm went off!*

I slashed at the tears leaking from my eyes and stared out at the busy city traffic, wishing for the millionth time my life was different. That *I* was somehow different. But we are creatures of habit, and are who we're born to be. This *was* me—the real Gabrielle Hargreave. And as disgraceful and abhorrent it felt to accept the idea, it didn't make the situation any less true.

You reap what you sow, Gabrielle.

Yeah, I'd learned my lesson the hard way.

BEN called to check on me as soon as he saw the news on TV about the National Gallery being evacuated. I wasn't surprised about the call, or the fact he knew something was up with me the minute he heard my voice. When he asked me if I was okay, I lied to my dear and caring friend. I lied and told him I was just upset about the possibility of a trove of priceless art being destroyed in a bomb blast, and further justified my "mood" about how fucked up the world was today with lunatics terrorizing in so many parts of the globe.

I was pretty sure he bought my story because he let it drop, but I couldn't be certain. Benny was very perceptive, and he knows me well. He forced an agreement out of me to have dinner with him the following week. Ben was, quite simply, digging for information and figured if he couldn't get anything out of me over the phone, he'd have more success in person. I loved him for it, though. Benny Clarkson was a rare gem of a person. We'd met at university photography class, gotten to know each other when we'd partnered together. As soon as I'd figured he wasn't trying to put the moves on me, my walls went down and I made a dear, dear friend. I don't know if he was more in tune with women because he was a gay man, or if it was just a connection we'd formed, but he sure understood me. Ben was very close to Brynne, too. He was like our older, protective brother who loved us unconditionally, always keeping an eye out.

As soon as we hung up, I shot a text to Brynne to let her know I was home. She hit me right back saying they were on the road to Somerset. Ethan was taking them to the countryside for a weekend away at his sister's historic mansion, which she runs as an exclusive bed and breakfast. The bomb threat had convinced him to leave tonight instead of tomorrow.

Made sense. Ethan Blackstone was as serious about protecting Brynne as he was in love with her. Pity the fool who ever tried to get close enough to hurt her.

My dad was next to check in, which was as predictable as Ben's call. The men in my life loved me, making their behavior easy to forecast. Can't say I minded that though.

"You're home already then?"

"Oh yeah, they kicked us out and I saw no point

in sticking around. I caught a cab and decided to call it an early night," I said smoothly.

My father is MetPol. Or in English, London Metropolitan Police. Chief Superintendent, in fact, and in charge of the Southwark division at New Scotland Yard. I am painfully aware he's heard every lie and bullshit story ever put out for public consumption. He knows very well what I study in school. He knows the focus of my master's program is the paintings of Tristan Mallerton. If art museums were being targeted for bombs, and I was working anywhere near then he would be all over it like white on rice. I know how his thought processes work. Having a cop for a father, I'd learned a few things through the years. Protecting me from harm was his number one priority.

"I sent Thorne over there to find you, and when he checked in to let me know you weren't there, I worried, darling. You should've made contact," he scolded me gently.

"I did, sort of. I waved to one of the security at Blackstone who knows me and let him see I was out of the building."

Silence.

"And, you don't have to send Desmond chasing after me every time, Dad."

That last jab got me a heavy sigh, and I knew

why. Desmond Thorne was my father's unfailing answer to his paternal worries about me. A superintendent on the rise at Scotland Yard, and just perfect for me, according to my dad. Yep, Dad made no secret about how much he approved of Detective Superintendent Thorne as boyfriend-slash-husband-slash significant other, for me, either. Whatever name you put to it, Desmond was the man for the job in the eyes of my father.

It was hard too, because I did like Des. A bit on the serious side but he was easy on the eyes, and he wasn't an ass. I'd give him props for making an effort with me. He'd made his interest known, and I wasn't an idiot. I'm sure if I'd given him even the slightest bit of encouragement, I could have him any way I wanted, as often as I liked. Visions of sweaty sex appeared in my head and I closed my eyes in an attempt to push them back.

Now it was my turn to sigh, for this was the heart of my problem.

I couldn't give in to those normal kinds of wants and desires that most girls have. Having a husband and two-point-four kids wasn't in *my* future, no matter how much my dad wanted it for me, or how much Desmond Thorne would be willing to fulfill the role of making it happen for me, either. *Let's not be greedy, Gabrielle. You've used up your allotted credits.*

Tonight's fresh hell had showed me, yet again, how much that was true.

"I don't want you going back there until the whole place has been given the all clear," my dad said firmly, probably in an effort to change the topic.

Not a problem. Hell, I doubted if I'd ever be able to go into the National Gallery again and not think about what I'd done with a complete stranger.

"I won't, Daddy."

"That's my good girl. I can't have you putting yourself at risk. Think what your mum would've had to say to me about it."

"Yeah…," I managed to whisper.

Just the mention of her made a raw wave of pain rush at me. I struggled to hold back the flood ready to spill over.

"Now I've upset you, my darling, and I am so sorry." My dad was straight-up hard line with most things, but when it came to his kids, and even the memory of my mother, he was very tenderhearted. He was a wonderful parent to me, and the fault wasn't anything he did wrong.

Nothing other than the fact he wasn't a woman. He wasn't a mother. He wasn't *my* mother.

My dad was a brilliant father, but sometimes a girl just needed her mom, and right now really felt like one of those times.

Priceless

"It's okay, Dad. I just miss her and sometimes I need someone to talk to abou—I mean—I just wish I could ask her for some advice—" I stopped blabbering, realizing how hurtful my words sounded. I didn't mean to make him feel bad, but I'm sure I just had.

"And I'm no substitute, am I?" he asked quietly.

"No—Dad, it's not you at all. You're always there for me, and you always have been. I love you and you're all I've got."

"That's never true, Gaby. You have your sister and brother, and your mum is still watching over all of you from heaven as she always will be."

"I know—"

"And it's normal for you to miss her, darling. I am very aware I'm just a useless old man but I *am* capable of listening…and I want you to know you can come to me to talk about anything at all. I might still be totally useless to you, but I do love you and want you to be happy."

"I know you do, Dad. And you're never useless. Forget what I said before. I'm the one that's useless right now. I think I need to get more sleep." I tried to make light of my situation.

"Now there's something I can endorse. Get more sleep and I'm sure you'll feel a great deal better in no time."

Right, Dad. More sleep is so going to help me with my "problem."

Spoken like a true man. I'd given him an out and he grabbed onto it as quickly as he could. My poor father was trying to be a rock of support to me, but he just didn't have the right equipment, a vagina of course, to do it.

He did everything well, but again, he was a man, and he was not my mom.

Despite his sweet offer to help me unburden my worries, if he knew the real reason for my depression right now, then "sweet" would be the last thing my dad was. He would want Mr. Ivanhoe's balls and probably his neck, too. Repeatedly.

There are many things I can share with my father, but tonight's escapade was definitely *not* one of them.

And my tears were just that much closer to spilling over.

I hauled myself into the shower after saying goodbye to him. As soon as I was under the warm spray, I let the tears loose in a torrent that did little to cleanse the stains that shone on my soul. I had been weak tonight just as I had been weak before. Nothing much had changed in me. I was still the same.

And that dirt just wasn't coming off.

MY roommate was annoyingly early the following morning when she called. I woke feeling like the zombie apocalypse had found me in the night. Becoming a zombie might just be the answer to my prayers, I thought wryly.

"Hello?" I managed, fumbling to silence the shrill of Brynne's ringtone drilling into my frontal lobe, having to do it by touch since my eyes weren't going to function until I got my reading glasses on.

"You won't believe what I'm staring at," she gushed.

"Do you know what time it is—because I sure do and I'm sure it's time for me to be sleeping."

"Sorry, Gab, but I had to. You would be drooling if you could see this…oh…midcentury *Mallerton* looming not a foot from me. I could rub my hands all over it if I wanted to."

"Better not do that, Bree. Tell me," I demanded, suddenly somewhat interested in the topic that thrust me into wakefulness.

"Well, it's probably about seven feet by four, and gorgeous as hell. A family portrait of a blonde woman and her husband, and their two children, a boy and a girl. She's wearing a pink gown and pearls that look like they belong in the Tower's crown jewels collection. He looks like he's in love with his wife. God, it's beautiful."

My mind started processing what she described but it didn't sound familiar to me. "Hmmm, I can't place it offhand. Can you ask if it's all right to take a picture and send it to me?"

"I will, as soon as I meet someone I can ask."

"Can you make out his signature?"

"Of course. It was the first thing I looked for. Bottom right, *T. Mallerton* in those distinctive block letters of his. It is, without a doubt, the real deal."

"Wow." I tried to imagine what she'd just described and wished I could see.

"Is everything okay with you? Last night was insane and I never saw you after that alarm went off. I wasn't feeling well and Ethan was in high-stress mode from some other stuff that happened."

"Like what other stuff?"

"Umm, not really sure yet. Some weird message on my old phone came through when Ethan had it on him. The person sent a crazy text and the song from…ah…that video they made of me."

"Shit, are you serious?" I felt for my friend. She'd been through hell because her douchebag boyfriend from years ago happened to be the son of the new running mate of the anticipated next United

States president. Her ex had made a disgusting sex tape of them back when they were teenagers, and now Brynne was a potential target, because nobody wanted that video to resurface. Not the senator candidate, and not Brynne either. That video had nearly destroyed her at one time. Her boyfriend, Ethan Blackstone, ran a security company and had her well protected now, but I could only imagine how paranoid he was after the bomb threat last night, and now some creepy anonymous text to Brynne's phone.

"Yep. I am afraid so," she said dismissively.

"No wonder Ethan was stressed, Bree. Why aren't you?"

"I don't know. I just want to believe nobody is after me and that this is just some kind of blip on the radar that will go away when the election is over. Trust me, Ethan is all over it."

"Yeah, well, it's good someone is," I grumbled.

"Hey," she asked, "you didn't answer my question. Are you okay? Last night was so messed up. I know we exchanged texts and no damage done, but still…"

I didn't know what to say to her. And the truth was I wasn't okay. I couldn't very well tell her I'd gotten busy with a hot guy I'd never met before. She'd be horrified as she should be, and I just couldn't make her uncomfortable by sharing. Brynne was too sensitive and sweet and she just wouldn't know what to do with information like that.

"Gabrielle?"

"I'm fine, really. No worries."

"Where did you go? I wanted to introduce you to Ethan's cousin, but that obviously never happened." She sounded slightly annoyed with me.

"I got…distracted, and then—then that alarm went off and I had to get out just like everyone else. Neil saw me and knew I'd made it out safely. And once we were outside the building there was nothing to do but stand around, so I grabbed the first cab I could and went home. I just wanted a shower and my bed. It was a weird night."

"You're so right about that."

"Benny called, too. He saw it on the news and was worried about us. I talked to him for a long time. Really, Bree, I am fine," I stressed, hoping she bought my story.

"Okay…if you say so." She didn't sound very convinced.

"I do want to meet Ethan's cousin with the old paintings someday, though. Maybe you can arrange it," I said by way of a peace offering.

"Yeah, maybe. Listen, I gotta go, Gab. Someone is here. I'll talk to you later and I'll see what I can do about sending a pic of the Mallerton. Love ya."

"Love ya back."

I powered off my phone after I said goodbye to Brynne. I needed to.

It was time for some serious introspection of my life. I couldn't afford to allow myself to go off on an emotional bender right now. I had school and work to occupy my time, and as for family, well, there was plenty to focus on there, too.

My sister Danielle still lived in Santa Barbara and went to school there despite our dad wanting her to come live in London like I had done. I wished she would, too. I worried about her there without us because I suspected she wasn't telling me everything that was going on. I had nobody I could really reach out to for accurate information, either. Our mom, Jillian, had lived in Santa Barbara with her husband, a man I refused to acknowledge as my step-father, until her sudden death three years ago. A man who wanted to get his claws into my sister and me, just as he had done to our mother. Garrick Chamberlain was no father of mine, and I didn't trust him further than I could throw him. Which was not at all.

But he was the father of my nineteen-year-old brother, Blake.

If I called him to ask about Dani or Blake, he'd

just guilt me into a tailspin for leaving and living in London when I should be home in the US where I belonged with my family. It wasn't the true reason he wanted me home, but it didn't matter to me. I didn't allow Garrick to influence me, ever. Or at least I gave it my very best shot not to let him into my orbit.

My mother and father were married for only three years. They met at a Peter Gabriel concert when she'd lived in London with her diplomat parents who'd been assigned to the embassy there. They'd fallen into a passionate romance, which I suspect was something from which neither of them ever fully recovered. I was born when she was just nineteen, and I'm sure only because she never told her parents she was pregnant until it was too late for an abortion.

My grandparents may not have been able to stop me from being born, but they made sure my mom and dad never got the chance to make a life together. My grandmother swept my mom and me back to Santa Barbara and out of my dad's influence until the marriage quietly ended. She was pregnant with my sister when she left England. Dani and I probably would never have had a chance to really know our dad if my grandparents hadn't been killed in a car accident when I was six. My dad started enforcing his visitation after they were gone, and we began spending our school holidays in London with him. When we were little, his mother, my Granny Anne, helped him with us when we came to England to stay. I've always imagined how remarkable it was for my dad to have gone above and beyond in being a parent to two tiny girls when it must have been so scary for him trying to do it all alone, and while living on another continent to boot.

The death of my mother's parents was the catalyst that changed our lives and set the path, though. My mother inherited their money, property, everything. That new-found wealth attracted the interest of a small-time Hollywood producer, Garrick Chamberlain.

I felt a stab of pain right in the gut and tried not to bring up the wretched past again. I told myself not to give into weakness, and not to allow the mistakes I'd made rule me. *You're stronger than that, Gabrielle. You make your choices and you control your own future now.*

Easier said than done.

I sighed instead and reached for the card propped on my nightstand. I'd received it three years ago, only a week before she passed away suddenly and unexpectedly. I ran my fingers over the front image of a beach at sunset on the beautiful handmade paper. My mom had done sweet things like that out of the blue. Sent me a card just to tell me she was thinking about me and how much she loved me.

I brought it up to my nose to sniff the paper. It still carried the scent of jasmine and sea grass. My mom had always loved to buy unconventional things like scented greeting cards and artsy trinkets. She'd sent me a wire bracelet with a painter's palette and paintbrush charm along with the card, too. The bracelet was lovely but, of course, it was her words that will always mean the most to me. I reached for my glasses so I could read it again.

Darling,

I know you're deep into your studies right now and just wanted you to receive some love and encouragement from me. I miss you all the time but I know you are doing so many amazing things over in London and in school. Your father does send updates when he can, so I know you've been through some hard exams recently. If you get any time, I hope you'll consider a visit. I so want to get you in my arms again and I know Dani and Blake do, too. I don't think I would let go of you for at least a day. Gaby, I know you feel guilt for things that happened in the past, but you shouldn't, my darling. You are a beautiful and remarkable young woman who did nothing more than countless other women have done since time immemorial. You know I believe there isn't anything that can't be overcome with determination and maybe some time. I would love to see you for any length of time you could spare. Just say the word and I'll see that tickets are arranged for you. If you can't, I understand, and will simply continue to love you from home. When I take a stroll on the beach at dusk I think of you and the wonderful talks we used to have, just the two of us discussing the mysteries of the universe. I know I would miss you whether you were in London or Los Angeles. Distance is just a number after all. I'm so grateful you have your father there to look out for you.

Love you always and forever,
Mom

For the millionth time, I tried not to read more into the letter than was there. That she'd wanted me to come home for a visit was apparent. But, was the reason more to do with her illness than just a longing to see her child? This was my worry and I knew I'd never know the answer. I'd called her and we'd talked for a long time after I'd received the card. She'd assured me she was just feeling lonely for me when she wrote it, and to please not worry.

That had been hard to do, though.

Of course I'd worried. My mom had been sick

with a chronic illness that had the potential to kill her, and married to a man who probably didn't mind if it did.

And then she did die.

It happened very quickly and without warning, because her general prognosis had not been dire. But the worst part was I'd not been able to get home in time to see her again. This card in my hand right now held the last words I would ever "hear" from my mother.

I pressed my eyes shut and thought of her. Of how good she was, and how determined she was to let me know how much she loved me in spite of what I'd done. It was my mother who had reached out to my dad and suggested I leave home and come to London to live where he could help me to find my way. After the mess I'd made, I'd needed some help. The two of them had kept an open line of communication about their children over the years, and I often wondered if Garrick hadn't snatched up my mother and married her, would my parents have gotten back together in time?

That had been impossible with my step-dad in the picture. He was also Blake's father and thus, I was stuck with Garrick Chamberlain as a family connection whether I liked it or not.

Garrick was solicitous of my mom when they

were together, but I'd never seen any evidence of the love affair between them. He'd married her for her money I was sure, and she had stayed married to him because of Blake. And now that she *was* gone, Garrick wanted to control even the portions of her estate that had been left to me and to Dani.

It was very easy for me to blame Garrick for everything. After all, my great shame was in part, because of him. Whenever I did visit my sister and brother in Santa Barbara, I couldn't wait to get away from Garrick and back home to London.

Home?

Where was my home, really?

I had family in London and in California, but I lived in London now. I couldn't see myself leaving it, either. There was too much back in California to hurt me. There was also nothing to tie my heart to California now my mom was gone. I missed Dani and Blake terribly, but for now my imperative was pretty simple.

Avoid the hurt at all costs.

Chapter 3

London
6th July

My do-over date with Maria would be handled a little differently than usual. We'd already met face to face, and so the typical dinner or date activity wasn't really necessary. We could get down to what we'd started the other night. No need to drag out the inevitable. I was contracting for sex and she was providing it.

Business.

Just contractual business and nothing more.

So why did I feel like shit about the fact I paid for a shag?

The truthful answer to that question helped me to realize my glass was empty and in desperate need of a refill.

I shrugged off my ugly thoughts as I mixed the Bombay and Schweppes, tossed in a lemon twist, and envisioned how Maria would look today when she showed up instead. To be honest, I couldn't wait to see her again. There was something about her that had got to me the other night despite our untimely interruption. I knew one thing for certain.

I wanted to be with her badly, and that fact alone was unusual for me.

Mostly, I couldn't stop thinking about her, or how she'd been so willing in my arms when I'd had her pinned against that gallery door with my fingers inside her. Maria was a born sexual submissive, I would bet my life on it, and I wanted to explore her further.

I felt my cock punch out when the buzzer went off. Maria was here, just on the other side of the door to my flat.

Mmmm…where to begin with her…was the delicious thought that slid through my mind as I put my hand on the knob and turned it.

I stared at the female before me wearing black stilettos paired with a pink and black trench coat cinched in tight at her waist with a bow. Probably the only thing standing between her and public indecency I imagined.

"Mr. Ivanhoe?" the too-thin blonde inquired softly. She was probably evaluating my frown and general puzzlement at her presence.

"But you're not Maria." I tilted my head at her.

"No, but please call me Maria if you wish," she answered with a nod as she checked me over with a smile. "I am here for your pleasure, Mr. Ivanhoe."

I guess she misread my shock at her not being whom I was expecting and took it for an invitation, because she swept inside and shut the door behind her. She walked into my living room and set her bag down on the coffee table. She turned back toward me and started unknotting the belt of her coat. The look in her dark brown eyes was predatory as she pulled the fabric of her belt out of the bow with a rasping draw.

Well, fuck.

This was definitely not who I'd been with in that store room. Not even close.

The lush goddess with the green eyes that had seduced me with her melting cries against my lips as I made her come, wasn't here with me after all. I couldn't remember more crushing disappointment than I felt in the moment.

I didn't enjoy the sex, not really.

When my guest opened the coat and revealed what was underneath I might have had enough to motivate me to see this through, but my heart wasn't in it.

Not when she dropped to her knees and wrapped her painted pink lips around my cock. And not when she sucked me off while pretending to love it. She hated sucking cock as much as Viviana had. I could tell.

She didn't mind the fucking though. Yeah, as much as I wasn't into her, I still managed to get her off and go through the motions. I would be double fisting my drinks afterwards I decided.

The whole thing was messy and less than satisfying.

And it took too long to get her out of my house after I was done with her.

Donadea, Northern Ireland
5th August

"YOU'RE just not telling me words I want to hear right now, Paul. Sorry, friend, but no. I need this shit out of my goddamned house and I need it gone now!" The pause from him was to be expected, and

I was more than used to it. In fact, this kind of reaction from others was pretty damn typical. I bark, and people move. Things get done the way they're supposed to and the way I want.

Well, in theory they do.

Waiting for Paul Langley to respond on the other end of the line made me impatient and I started tapping the top of my desk. I studied the worn oak grain of the wood and realized something I'd never really thought about before. My ancestors must have sat here at this same desk. Even as far back as maybe two hundred years ago I supposed. But that didn't change the fact that it was *still* just a desk. A useful piece of furniture. A tool to be utilized rather than just on display as a formal antique appreciated only for its aesthetic value.

"Hello? You still there?"

"I wouldn't call it shit, Ivan."

"Right. Let me rephrase it for you then. Paul, would you please get someone over to my house capable of archiving the very valuable shit I have a great abundance of? A graduate student perhaps? There must be someone who needs a job. The papers tell of gloom and doom for the pissing dreadful economy. A starving artist? Work with me here, please. I do plenty for your organization and you know it."

Langley sighed heavily into the phone. "I'll see what I can do. There may be a possible candidate, but I'm not sure. The student I've in mind is very busy and scheduling may be a problem." He hesitated before letting me have it. "And you aren't the easiest person to…ah…work for."

"Are you trying to tell me I'm an arsehole?"

Langley laughed softly. "Yes. And I couldn't pass up the chance to admit it to you either, especially since you asked."

"Nothing new there. Right. Good. So offer your student a massive sum of my quid. I pay well. Get someone over here to do the job and you'll get your usual toward the philanthropic health of the arts and all that crap, and I won't be drawn and quartered for letting priceless paintings go to rot."

He muttered something about expecting a bigger donation cheque this year if he managed to find someone to come out. "See that you do and you just might," I told him as we ended the call.

I sent off an email to my assistant in London telling him to follow up with Langley per our conversation. Lowell would keep this item current and remind me again if no word came from Langley soon about assigning me a student from U of L. Gratefully I had some good people working hard for me.

Once I finished that business my eyes wandered around this stately room I'd inherited, to study the rich paneling carved by some master craftsman eons ago, over the valuable paintings hung atop it, past the antique furniture and the personal items which had belonged to my ancestors, to finally rest upon the best part of the whole room in my opinion. The view out the floor-to-ceiling window. The landscape of Donadea was stunning in all its green lushness—hills and dales dotted with trees contrasting against the blue skies above. Too bad I didn't have the heart to enjoy it much. Not anymore.

I'd loved coming here as a kid even after Mum died. The best times of all had been the long breaks in summer. Riding, shooting, fishing, times at the lake, picnics. I'd learned to fly here. It had been magical. A place to forget the harsh bustle of London and the many responsibilities that came with this blasted life I'd inherited. But Viviana had taken even the peace of this sanctuary from me. Now Donadea reminded me of all that I didn't have, which was symbolic for why I wanted this place cleared out.

The time had come to let the past go.

It didn't serve me in any good way and I didn't need any more bad. I'd had enough in my thirty-four years to last for a while. I didn't like to complain about my life because it would sound incredibly ingenuous to anyone who might be inclined to quote me. Which they would do with the utmost glee. I could see the Fleet Street rags headlining me now— SUICIDE WATCHES FOR LORD IVAN.

I had money, of course, and fame to an extent. Infamous was more like it. I had some Olympic medals and even a coveted gold. I'd been born with the right name mostly. And because of the untimely deaths of others, I had so much when so many had so little. So yeah, I couldn't complain about anything to anybody. I could only bear the hand I'd been dealt. Which sucked.

I left my study and walked across the west wing of the house to the portrait gallery. The walls were filled. There was too much here. It needed to be sorted and some maybe sold, donated, or stored for preservation even. I thought of the ironic twist of fate that had left me as caretaker of such goods. An art collection to rival the best in the world and I knew next to nothing about it.

My uncle Matthew, the twelfth Baron Rothvale, had not been much better, and my father? Fuck no, and fuck no a hundred times after that. His interests had been all over the place for the short time he'd been in line for the helm of this slowly leaking vessel. This estate had never belonged to him anyway, and that one small fact pleased me the most. Irony was cruel most of the time.

I took one last look around the room before going right back out again. No, the paintings in this house had been neglected for a great many decades and they were due some greatly needed attention. Even my ignorant arse knew that.

It was my desire to get the project started and then leave the expert to finish it. I shouldn't have to stay here indefinitely, even though the thought of staying at Donadea was very appealing, besides I had work in London that required me there regardless. Always.

Work, or trying to stay off the paparazzi grid—something I never quite managed to do for very long.

The Olympics had gone off without a hitch until just after they wrapped. The events ran smoothly, and my commentator's contract had actually been a refreshing change of pace for me. The Games were a smashing success despite Great Britain's team performance on native soil in the archery competition. I'd loved every moment of it. Nobody had set off any bombs and I was still in one piece. Just when I'd felt like I might take a breath and let my guard down for two seconds, more shit was dredged up.

A ridiculous assumption on my part, of course,

because my absence in the trash presses couldn't be tolerated for more than a month before something sordid needed to be fed to the inquiring public. I sold them fuckloads of papers. I often wondered what my rank was on their "favorites" list. I had to be top five.

The blonde in the trench coat who'd come to my flat had been bought by somebody, and when she'd set down her bag on my coffee table, it'd been a strategic placement. A good portion of the blow job had made it onto video. And really, who should give two shillings about whom I fuck? Or how? But apparently some did.

The gossip headlines had been brutal and getting it taken down had cost me a horrifying amount of brass. Again. This fucking crap was becoming status quo for me.

The incognito escort service was off my list, too. I didn't have a choice about that. They'd been compromised and my privacy couldn't be guaranteed anymore. I'd miss the sex, but I'd survive. One doesn't need to fuck in order to live. It's nice, but not a necessity.

I knew what would make me feel a little better, though, so I headed outside for the field targets, stopping to collect my beloved Kodiak Recurve and a quiver on the way. I'd never be able to stop my shooting completely, and hopefully would never have to. The freshness of this place, the stillness, the peace, the goodness… It was what I needed more than any other thing.

I told myself this was the reason I'd abandoned London to come over to Donadea. But who was I fooling? This time of year was always the same for me. I had to get away from everything that reminded me of the past, and this was the only place I had left to go to where that was even possible.

10ᵗʰ August

THE sun was starting to dim when I decided I might as well admit to myself I was lost.

Really lost.

The perfect metaphor for just about everything in regards to my life.

I pulled to the side of the road and looked at the directions I'd printed out from my computer. Trouble was, this was a huge estate and most of the roads were unmarked, meandering peacefully in all directions over the rolling green. The GPS that came with the rental in Belfast wasn't worth a damn in places like this. It was likely to have me driving over a cliff if I depended on it.

The words blurred together on the paper anyway. My reading glasses were in my suitcase, which was sitting in the trunk of the car, where they could do me absolutely no good at the moment, of course. My night vision sucked, so I was screwed there, too. I fumbled for my cell phone and dialed the number Professor Langley had given me.

After several rings voice mail picked up. "Everley. Leave a message." The voice was curt and clipped, somewhat cold. No greeting. No other information offered. Nothing to make me feel even the slightest bit comfortable about showing up for a job at a gloomy Irish manor house, filled to the brim with god knows what. I highly doubted it would work anyway.

I was only here as a favor to Paul Langley, one of my academic advisors at the University of London. He'd pulled me into his office and basically said if I wanted to be recommended for the M.Phil. in Art History, then it would be prudent of me to accept this appointment, and thereby, please the patron. Professor Langley was fair, but he could be tough, too. He'd told me there was a substantial amount of funding riding on this job and that there was nobody better to take it on. Paul Langley was also on the boards for every art society known to man. One did not tell him no. Not if I wanted to get a job in my field someday. And apparently one did not tell Mr. Everley "no" either.

"This is Gabrielle Hargreave from the University of London. I—I'm having some trouble with the directions to find your place. It's getting dark. I suppose. I'm lost. Please call me back." I left my message and sank down in the driver's seat. I figured the best thing to do was wait for someone to return my call. All of those survival shows always said so. If you are lost, stay put until someone finds you.

The sun slowly dipped below the horizon in a gorgeous display of red and purple. I watched the whole thing and waited. And waited some more. Nobody called me back. I checked for messages every few minutes but it remained silent. The idea of spending the night in this car, afield in the Irish countryside did not appeal to me either. How on earth had I ended up in such a mess?

I called the number again and left another message. I hoped my voice didn't sound too pathetic on the recording. God, didn't the man have some servants? He was an earl or a viscount or something, according to Professor Langley. Didn't they have staff at their beck and call to handle every little problem that arose? How much longer would I have to wait out here in the dark? And it was getting colder. I needed the loo. Trying to get a handle on my rising panic, I got out of the car, opened the trunk and unzipped my suitcase.

My jacket would be a good start. For August, the weather was mostly mild but this was Northern Ireland and I was pretty confident rain was imminent. And of course, the temperature always dropped with the sun even if it did set late in summer. I retrieved my glasses, and put them in my pocket.

Truth be told, I didn't feel at all well. I had a headache starting and my muscles felt stiff and achy. I prayed I wasn't coming down with something vile. I couldn't afford to be sick right now and try to do this favor for Professor Langley. Just—no.

Scanning the landscape, I looked for anything that might resemble a manor house. Nothing. It was so dark now that the only light was from the risen moon, glowing serenely above the fast-moving clouds. If I didn't want to get soaked I needed to get back in the car. I might as well start driving again, too. Enough of this "staying put" bullshit. It was getting me literally nowhere. The dark, the rain, and the morose feelings of helplessness matched my life perfectly at the moment.

Chapter 4

I felt my jaw twitching as I checked my watch. This was bloody irritating and then some. Next, I re-read the email Lowell had printed out for me for the third time. **Gabriel Hargreave will be driving in from Belfast today to assess your collection. –Paul Langley**

Well, whoever Gabriel Hargreave was, he certainly couldn't tell time. Or know how to use a telephone. *Useless artsy twit.*

I'd stayed home purposefully this evening in order to be here to greet the student Langley had found for my archival work. So far, Hargreave didn't impress me in the slightest.

I was convinced that young people today didn't have the drive to be successful. No initiative. Little commitment. It was pathetically shameful what I had to put up with. I refilled my drink and went to the window to look for the possibility of headlamps coming up the drive. Nothing. What a waste of time. The twit was probably one of those Bohemian art students who lived life on a whim with no idea whatsoever of keeping to a schedule or the job he'd agreed to. The job I was paying him to do. Christ, what did it take to get some help around here?

Seeing my mobile blinking on the sofa, I went over to retrieve it, realizing I must've set it down when I was watching ESPN earlier. I had a bad habit of doing that.

I checked and saw three new messages. I didn't know what I expected but what I got was not it.

Shit! My grad student, who sounded very feminine, was lost and off the road in the dark apparently. I checked my watch again and grimaced. The first call had been left nearly three hours ago and it was black outside now. I grabbed my car keys and headed for the garage, hitting redial as I went.

A tremulous voice answered on the third ring. "Hello?"

"Is this Gabriel Hargreave?" I asked. "Where are you? I can come down in the Rover and collect you or at least lead you up the proper road." I tried to keep the harshness from my voice. I didn't want him to quit, *before* I could fire him at any rate.

"Not Gabriel, I'm Gabrielle. Gabrielle Hargreave. And how the hell should I know where I am? I told you I'm lost. And it's dark out here."

"Oh, my bad, *Gabrielle,* you've been driving around with no idea where you're going for three hours?" I was pretty shocked by what she'd just told me. "Why on earth would anyone continue driving while they're lost in the dark? You're supposed to stay put and wait for help. Didn't you ever watch a survival show?"

"Nobody came and I thought I could find my way," she wailed into my ear. "It's raining and I just drove through a stream across the road." She sounded hysterical now, and I couldn't help wincing as I moved my mobile away from my ear.

I tried to adopt a patient tone. "But I cannot come and collect you if you keep driving around." Dead silence greeted me, and I wondered if I'd had lost connectivity for a moment, until I heard her breathing. "What landmarks can you see?"

A muffled sob came through loud and clear, and I felt a moment's guilt for not catching her calls, when she actually rang for help. I really needed to stop setting my mobile down in random places—

"I already told you before, I can't see a bloody thing!" she blasted back at me.

"Well, you need to calm down, Miss Har—"

"Wait! I can make out the profile of some low hills to my right. And there's nothing but fields to my left. I swear I can hear waves crashing below me. Please say you know where I am!"

Was she crying? Unease started to settle in my gut. Maybe this person was not cut out for the job after all. "Are you outside of your car? I think I can find you but you need to hang on and get back in your car. Turn on your headlamps and whatever the hell else you do, for the love of Christ, stop driving and wait for me."

I headed out in the Rover, glad for the four wheel drive over country roads that had turned to slopping mud. She'd sounded frantic. The part about hearing waves crashing below her did not sit well either. There were sections of the cliff side where a person could simply slip over if they were not aware of their bearings. And Miss Hargreave was certainly not going to be the poster girl for Outdoor Enthusiast anytime soon, I could safely wager.

The drive was slow going due to the rain and mud until I got to the main road. I traversed that for a good two kilometers before turning off again, for where I thought she might be. When headlamps came into view I breathed out a heavy sigh in relief and pulled up alongside what I assumed was her Volkswagen.

The economy did not look promising for making it up the muddy road tonight. I came up to the driver's window and looked in. Where was she?

"Miss Hargreave?" I called out.

Only the sound of rain and the rumble the windscreen wipers from the Rover filled the darkness.

OH dear God, he was here.

I'd seen the lights of the Range Rover as soon as it pulled up alongside my rental but I couldn't just pop out to greet my new boss with my jeans around my ankles, now could I? I'd needed the loo hours ago and my bladder was past the point of negotiation.

Far, far past.

The tree I'd chosen to shield my privacy was an ancient thing, and as soon as I was restored to my former self, I called out to the tall form bent over, peering into the window of my car. "I'm over here. Mr. Everley? That is you, right?"

His head whipped around so fast it gave me a moment's pause and I stumbled.

"Of course it's me. Who else would it be? What in the hell are you doing hiding under a tree? Why aren't you waiting for me in your car where it's dry?" Mr. Everley sounded very annoyed. Like an asshole, too.

"I had—I needed to—I was desperate for a loo if you must know." Seriously, did he talk to everyone this way? It wasn't like I'd tried to get lost or that I was actually responsible for the torrential summer rain.

The stiffness of my legs combined with the mud, the cold, and the general awkwardness of this whole situation did not help me with my balance one bit.

I slipped again and went down on my ass in the sticky mud, right at Mr. Everley's feet.

A large hand reached down to help me up. "You'll get mud all over my leather seats now," he said blandly.

I took his offered hand and let him haul me up. "No, I won't. I'll follow you in my car." I was so mortified at this point, walking in the mud and the rain sounded like a damn good idea. Closed inside a vehicle with my new boss scowling and growling at me, with mud all up my backside? So out of the question.

Mr. Everley took one sneering look at my car and shook his head at me. "That little thing will die a muddy death if you try it. You don't have a choice. Get in." He certainly had no trouble ordering me around. Must be the duke or earl in him.

I stood there for a moment and hoped for a miracle. The rain kept falling and my boss kept glaring. I swallowed and gestured toward my car. "My things. My equipment. To do the work, I must have—"

"Tomorrow." He said it quietly, and in a way that brooked no argument. Christ, he was intimidating, and tall, but that was about all I could make out of him in his bulky rain jacket and ball cap. The dark, the rain, and my sucky night vision made it pretty difficult to see much of anything. I mostly just wanted to get under a dry roof.

He shifted and folded his arms across a wide chest. "Miss Hargreave, do you enjoy standing in the cold night rain? Slithering around in the mud to piss behind a tree? Driving around aimlessly in the dark with no idea where you are headed? Because I can assure you that I do not care for any of those things. It's nearly eleven o'clock and I would like to greet my bed. Can we get you into my Rover so I may make this a possibility before it is indeed tomorrow?"

Ouch.

I was convinced I had no luck at all. Not one speck of it. This man *was* an asshole and I had somehow landed smack dab in the middle of my own personal hell, with him in the role of the devil. With horns. And cracking a whip.

I turned and wrenched my suitcase from the trunk of the rental car, hoping my equipment would be safe for the night, but really, it would be on him if anything happened to my stuff. He could deal with it.

Pompous jackass!

I marched alongside his Rover with the precious leather seats, tossed my bag in the back atop same said leather seats, and seated myself in front.

Mud? Meet expensive leather!

I was determined not to speak another word to *Lord Condemnation* if I didn't have to.

Jerk wad, massive pain in my ass!

MISS Hargreave was nothing like the grad student I had anticipated. She was a "she" for one thing, a great deal younger than I'd figured on, and from her body language, was quite enraged at the moment. I looked over at her sitting stoically in my front seat. Oh yes, she was steamed to the gills. Her arms were folded and the earthy scent of wet mud was all over her. She rather reminded me of a cat being given a bath, all claws and hissing. She had an interesting accent too.

"You're not native are you?"

She started to turn her head toward me but then she caught herself and kept herself facing out the window. She was punishing me for making her wait in the rain for three hours probably. There was something about her that seemed vaguely familiar but I couldn't place whatever it was.

"My accent blows my cover every single time. Damn."

Okay, she was more than a little wound up.

"American?"

"Yep."

The windscreen wipers sweeping back and forth pretty much filled the cold silence between us. I supposed my comment about pissing behind a tree had not been well thought out, and I wondered what she really thought of me. Probably something along the lines of, "Go fuck yourself, you sodding arsehole." Yeah, Miss Hargreave had some pluck in her it seemed, despite her harrowing evening.

"Look, I'm sorry about not getting your call when it first came through. I didn't have my mobile on me."

She kept herself turned away and facing out toward the dark wet night. "Doesn't matter. I'll be out of your hair in the morning." She gestured with an elegant hand. "This whole thing…is obviously not going to work." She snorted a laugh. "American art student cataloging nineteenth century Romanticist masterpieces for a British earl. What a joke! I'm in way over my head—"

"That's not true. I'm only a lowly baron, not even close to being an earl," I interrupted in hopes of distracting her from what was certain to be an emotional tirade, as well as her notice.

"My bad," she sneered, mimicking me from earlier. "I've got to work on my Debrett's Peerage as well as my navigation skills. I've got quite a list of improvements to tackle, don't I?" The sarcasm dripping off her was pretty harsh and she still spoke to the window.

Nope. Not distracted in the least.

I tried again. "So how does an American girl end up at University of London taking a graduate degree, and more to the point, how in the hell do you know Debrett's Peerage? Surely that's knowledge fit only for the natives." If distracting her didn't work, maybe teasing would.

She laughed. Just a short breath of air and a shake of her head, but it made me feel better. What I really wanted was to get a good look at her. I wanted to check Miss Hargreave out, and see what she was made of in a lighted room—sans wet mud preferably. If going by the rest of my impression of her, and the sound of her voice being any indication at all, I could be in for a lovely treat.

"You're not going to quit before you've even seen all the paintings I've got in my house, are you? Because, that would be a travesty. Well at least I think it would. I don't know shit about art."

She didn't move her position of staring out at the rain and I felt the sudden need to convince her to stay. Nothing about this night was going to plan. She wasn't going to be an easy sell, but I really needed someone for this job. It'd been left for about five decades too long. I required a professional, and there was one sitting in the seat next to me right now. A spitfire Yank with lousy directional sense, but an expert all the same.

I softened my voice. "I take that back. I know enough about art to know I need a professional's help."

She moved in her seat and sighed, just as I pulled

up to the garage and parked the Rover. She held out her hand and turned her body toward me.

"Shall we begin again? Gabrielle Hargreave, University of London. I'm the professional here to have a look at your art collection." She faced me now, but I still couldn't see her very well. I liked the sound of her voice though. It sounded…sexy.

The garage light had brightened the interior by a fraction where we sat together, and I finally got a glimpse, but could still barely make out her features. I felt surprise for the second time tonight as I closed my hand around hers for a firm shake. Gabrielle Hargreave was, again, so not what I was expecting.

Her hair was soaking wet and pulled back in a tie, but the overall impression was one of beauty. I may be a waste at social pleasantries but I do know when a woman is beautiful, and Miss Hargreave was certainly that.

I was changing my opinion about my new grad student rather quickly.

"Ahh, Gabrielle Hargreave, pleasure to meet you. Ivan Everley, inheritor of all this…and of course, shuttle driver for lost American art students." I smiled at her.

She dropped my hand and looked down at her lap.

"That bad?" I tilted my head down to try to get

her to look at me again. She seemed miserable.

"You forgot to add 'wet and caked in mud' to your description."

"Not really. I remembered the 'wet and muddy' but figured I was pushing my luck with the 'lost American' part already. I'm not a complete idiot, Miss Hargreave."

She arched a very pointed brow at me and I felt the hit right in the groin.

I reached for the door handle and got out of the Rover as fast as I could. This whole situation was getting a little awkward. We were bantering back and forth like we'd known each other for years rather than mere minutes.

But before I could make my way over to her side to open the door for her, she'd already exited and was bent over my leather seats earnestly attempting to remove the smudges of mud left on them from the backside of her jeans.

I got a very nice look at her from behind though and I wasn't complaining. Nope. Miss Hargreave had a fine looking arse attached to those mile long pins of hers. Covered in mud or not, it was a beauty.

I cleared my throat. "Shall we?"

"Sorry about your leather seats. I can come back and clean them tomorrow."

"No worries. Finnegan will take care of it," I

said as I pulled her bag from the backseat. "He's the man to see around here if you want anything done. I'll introduce you as soon as we get up to the house. On second thought, it's late now." I checked my watch. "He's probably gone to bed." I nodded. "Of which, you're no doubt in desperate need of yourself."

"I am exhausted," she mumbled, while stifling a yawn with her delicate hand.

I led her forward, my hand pressed against her back as we made our way out of the darkened garage. Again, I was struck with the overwhelming feeling of something I couldn't quite put my finger on. Odd, but I kept thinking that we'd met before in some capacity.

"This doesn't look nice at all," I said. The rain, which had been doing steady work up to this point, decided to unleash in biblical proportions. The sound of the drops hitting every surface as they poured down in sheets to rival Noah's flood, roared in front of us.

"Well I don't think I can get much wetter," she shouted over the noise.

"That's probably a good thing, because we're both about to find out. We've got to make a run for it!" I yelled, grabbing her hand and pulling her with me as I made for the safety of the house.

Chapter 5

Being dragged through a deluge along a dark path in unfamiliar territory was not my favorite, but having a guide who knew where he was going was so much better than none at all. At least I wasn't spending the night in a rental car at the bottom of a ditch.

We dashed toward a looming stone manor, Neo-Gothic design from what I could tell in the dark and streaming rain. I held onto Mr. Everley's hand and went forward. He pulled us through puddles and small lakes until we headed up some stone steps, and finally to a door that got my attention. It was a behemoth made of oak and carved with heavy designs of flora and fauna. Fascinating. I'd get a better look tomorrow in the light of day.

We entered through the door and into a mudroom of sorts. Perfect place for me. I was covered in the stuff, and could think only about getting it off me via a hot bath. A soft bed would be welcome, too. In the morning I could figure out what kind of art Mr. Everley had stashed away in his gloomy corner of Ireland and decide if his collection merited the work or not.

"Here, allow me," he said, taking my coat off my back and hanging it dripping on a peg.

"Thanks."

I tried to shake the water off my hands, attempting to sort out my appearance, which must be truly horrifying by now, but it was beyond hopeless. "I don't think I've ever been so soaking wet before." I brushed at my emerald-green shirt, realizing because my poor jacket had lost to the rain, I was soaked through to the skin.

"Yeah, it's downright evil tonight. I'm so glad you're not out there any longer because I fear you would've floated away by now, Miss Hargreave." He was busy hanging up his own coat and pulling off the ball cap he'd been wearing, when we both turned to face one another.

"I'm so grateful you finally checked your pho—"

In the light.

Where he could really see me.

And where I could really see him…for the first time.

But it wasn't the first time we'd seen each other.

Straight dark hair spilled down his neck. Lips that I remembered knowing how to kiss me, opened in total surprise. Captivating green eyes that had held onto mine in a crushingly intimate moment, widened in shock. Mr. *Ivanhoe* appeared to register the same horrible conclusion I was experiencing.

Those dark green eyes of his narrowed and glared down at me accusingly, looking fearsome and terrifying in what was, without a doubt, anger at finding me in his house.

Oh no, please, God, no! It just couldn't be *him* of all people.

I think it was safe to say we were both in shock.

He pointed a finger at me. "You!"

I stared up into his fuming eyes, frozen and horrified with only one thought racing through my mind.

Run away.

I tried to. I moved to turn my body away from him and flee, but he was too quick. Within a millisecond he had me gripped by the shoulders and facing him. I was going nowhere. Not that I had anywhere *to* go when I was lost and muddy somewhere in the wilds of Northern Ireland, in some old stone mansion with what was certainly a crazed madman.

"What in the fuck are you doing here? *Maria,* wasn't it?" he spat, shaking me with a hard jerk.

I shook my head and tried to flinch out from his iron grip on me. "W-who is M-maria?" I sputtered dumbly. "Paul Langley just sent me here to have a look at your p-p-paintings." I could feel my body quivering in complete terror and fear for my safety. What would he do to me? "Please…don't…hurt me," I begged on a whisper.

He blinked and released me instantly, as if he needed distance to keep his anger in check, and surprised at how hard he'd been holding onto my arms.

"The evidence from last time wasn't enough, was it? Even Langley's gotten in on things now?" He scoffed and looked disgusted with me, a sneer curling one side of his lip. "Were you planning on videotaping again or just photos this time?"

"What are you talking about?" I shook my head and tried to explain. "I'm not here to b-bother you, Mr. Everley, I—I'm just here to do my job."

"Was part of your job to fuck me for money?" he snapped back.

I wanted to crawl into a crack in the floorboards and die. "No! No, I—I didn't know who you were. It was a mistake—"

"—but you know who I am now, don't you, Miss Hargreave?"

I nodded slowly and mouthed a pitiful "yes." How was it possible I'd been with this man on the night of the gala and he was one and the same as Mr. Everley, the person whose paintings I was supposed to inventory? I was so mortified.

"And if that wasn't enough, now you're here at my house. My sanctuary. What do you really want? More money? My name can't be hauled through the mud any more than it already has been. I'll give you this, Miss Hargreave, or, Maria, or whatever the fuck you call yourself, you're certainly industrious for someone so young. Art conservationist *and* a private escort all in one tidy package. I'm suitably impressed, and that's saying something. I sure wish I'd found you a long time ago." He leered up and down my body, gesturing with his hands. "I bet you make more as an escort though, you're banging hot."

I couldn't believe my ears. Was he insane?

Hell, he wasn't the only one on the verge of insanity. I was alone out in the middle of nowhere with this deranged man with no way to leave. If he put his hands on me again I swear to God I was out the door, rainstorm or not.

"I am not an escort!"

He barked out a sarcastic laugh. "Really? You sure fooled me then."

"Wait—you think I work for an escort service?" I suddenly remembered back to that night and him saying something about the "service" contacting me…right before he dragged me into a side room and proceeded to make me lose all of my good sense. "You're dead wrong, Mr. Everley, because I am most certainly *not* an escort, nor have I ever worked for any kind of escort service. I'm an art student at U of L and I was at the National Gallery for the gala on behalf of the university that night. I thought you wanted a VIP patron tour." God, was I even having this conversation? Explaining to him how I wasn't a prostitute? I pressed my eyes shut. Surely I was deep into some kind of alternate reality dream state. Must be the lack of sleep. That had to be the answer to all of this.

I opened my eyes and saw he was still standing there glaring, the long dark hair I remembered, falling forward to frame the harsh set of his stubbly jaw.

Nope. Definitely not a dream.

He didn't believe me at all, I could tell that

much. Angry waves still emanated off his imposing form while I stood babbling about mistaken identity and praying I was indeed sleep-walking.

"That was one helluva tour, Miss Hargreave. In fact, I'd say you're a real pro at giving them. But wait," he paused, pointing one long finger upward and tilting his head, "our tour was interrupted just when it started to get good for me. Now that I reflect on it, I say you owe me the rest of your special...*tour*. I did pay after all. I should get value for my money, don't you think?"

He leaned in very close and brought the same pointed finger to just under my chin where he tipped it toward his lips. With just a few inches between us, I could feel the warmth of his body heat radiating between us, and see sparks blazing in his eyes. The tension penetrated, and I knew he'd moved well past taunting sarcasm with me. Mr. Everley was dead serious.

And just as devastatingly handsome as I remembered, which annoyed me greatly.

"Despite your rather rude intrusion into my private home, I find I'd still very much like to fuck you, Miss Hargreave."

He was also propositioning me for sex. *He was propositioning me for sex?*

I swallowed and felt myself go weak in the knees,

realizing I was in a potentially dangerous situation if he decided to force the issue. I had to get the hell out of here.

"Will I get the rest of my *tour* now?" he whispered darkly, with the conceited suggestion of an arrogant male who thought he might be getting lucky in a few. "Shall we do up a porno for everybody as well? Share it with the media? Does it gain you a bigger fee, Maria?"

I yanked my chin back from the press of his index finger. "That's not my name! And let me enlighten you, Mr. *Ivanhoe*, about precisely what's not going to be happening here with us tonight…or ever." I gestured my hand back and forth between us. "No sex."

His eyes widened and his mouth turned up in a smirk. "Not in the mood just yet after your ordeal?" He lowered his tone seductively. "I can help you get in the mood. Maybe you'd like to see some of my paintings first if art really is something that interests you." His smirk turned into a wicked grin that was all about lewd acts and dirty deeds. I could see exactly where he was going in his mind.

"Oh my God, you're so disgusting. You hired a prostitute to have sex with you at the Mallerton Gala and you thought I was her?" I shook my head slowly back and forth and touched my chest with my fist.

"So. Not. Her."

He cocked an aristocratic eyebrow at me. "You weren't complaining when I had my fingers buried in your cunt, or when you were coming all over my han—"

I slapped him as hard as I could across the face.

ONE thought filled my head and it was to get away from him.

I ran for the massive carved door and yanked it open. Streams of rain still poured in sheets from the portico. There was nowhere for me to get away *to*. No sanctuary for me to hide in. It was storming outside and nearing midnight in the middle of nowhere. I couldn't even say where I was, let alone tell anyone to come for me. I was as trapped here as if I was marooned on a desert island.

I shut the door against the elements and turned back around to see him standing there with his arms folded, a wide stance, and all traces of cockiness now absent from the face I'd just slapped. In its place was a cold calmness that left me with absolutely no idea of what he was going to do. Order me to leave? Send me back out into that storming hell? Ravish me anyway?

He spoke low and precisely, his meaning very clear, and brooking absolutely no argument.

"It appears you're staying here in this house whether you want it or not."

A sob escaped from my throat unwillingly.

"No need to worry, Miss Hargreave, you won't be bothered again tonight."

And then he just left me there and walked away. I heard his footsteps retreating, and watched him disappear as he moved off into another part of his house. The darkness swallowed him up...until I was alone in an unfamiliar old stone mansion with a storm raging outside its walls.

Rocky Horror Picture Show, anyone?

Eventually the sound of his steps faded until all I could hear was the pounding rain hitting the windows and the eerie brush of leaves scraping against the stone walls and glass windows from the wind whipping the trees around.

I wanted to be brave. I tried so hard not to cry, but I couldn't stop those bastard tears from leaking out. It was all just too much. Everything. The ordeal of getting lost would have been enough, but the revelation of meeting *him* again sent me right over the edge. How was it even possible? I took little comfort in the fact that his crude and obnoxious behavior cancelled out my shame and embarrassment, and then some. A prostitute? Really!?

I glanced around at my surroundings and drew in a deep shaky breath, hugging my arms tightly for strength. I could get through this one night, I told myself. I had shelter from the storm, and dry clothes in my suitcase. I had my phone and my wallet. And in the morning, I would figure out a way to get back to my rental car and down to the airport at Belfast.

I was going to be just fine.

There was some relief at knowing my immediate safety was secure—but it also gave me an excuse to indulge in a little self-pity.

I sat down on the old wooden bench in Mr. Everley's mudroom and wept like a baby.

THE sound of a throat clearing roused me from my desperation and told me I was no longer alone. I raised my eyes to see an older gentleman standing in the doorway of the mudroom. His hair was graying over what must have been red when he was younger, and he was wearing what looked to me like a 1950's smoking jacket that went all the way to the floor. Soft leather loafers peeped out from the burgundy silk edging and a patterned neck cloth tucked in around his throat. Quite the picture of distinguished country elegance.

From 1951.

It was also very clear he'd just been roused out of his bed, too. Was it possible for me to have caused any more disruption to this household than I had in the short time I'd been here? I didn't think so.

He looked me over, probably disgusted by my bedraggled state. Was this one of Mr. Everley's servants sent down to *deal* with me? I lifted my chin and tried to pretend he hadn't just caught me bawling my eyes out. What a joke that was. I slashed at the tears rolling down my face, and stood up quickly, trying to face up to whatever was in store for me.

His face gentled and he reached for my suitcase. "My name is Finnegan. May I show you to your room, Miss Hargreave, is it?" His voice had a definite Irish lilt, but refined, and strangely…kind.

"Y-yes…I g-g-guess so," I managed to answer. "It's j-just for the n-night. I'm leaving in the m-m-morning." It was nearly impossible for me to speak from the involuntary sobs that still had hold of me. I hoped I wasn't frightening the poor man to an early death.

"Follow me, my dear. You look like you could use some warming up…and drying off."

Thank God he took charge because I was very

near the end of my rope. I followed Mr. Finnegan with the burgundy smoking jacket down a hallway and up an impressive staircase, past enormous paintings and sculptures I refused to even try to make out in the dim lighting because I would never see them again after this night.

I know myself pretty well.

I just couldn't take in any more. Something dry to put on, a bed, and maybe a couple Nurofen if I was really lucky, and the sum total of my requirements would be mercifully fulfilled.

"This is the room we had arranged for your stay with us, Miss Hargreave. It is a suite with a sitting room just off there." He pointed to an open doorway lit by lamplight. "You'll also find things for making tea or coffee if you'd like a hot drink before you retire."

I looked around at the beautiful rooms set up for me to live in while I worked on assessing Mr. Everley's art collection, and at Mr. Finnegan regarding me so kindly as he explained the basics…and felt tears leaking down my face again.

I vaguely registered a conversation with him about helping me to get back to my rental car tomorrow so I could leave, amid more pathetic tears. He took it all in his stride and patted my hand awkwardly before he left me alone, saying something about breakfast in the morning, and that things would look better to me after a restful sleep. He probably thought I was an escapee from a mental ward, poor man.

Maybe things would feel better in the morning. Or maybe they wouldn't.

They probably wouldn't, I decided.

And by this point I didn't even care.

I didn't ponder Mr. Finnegan's predictions, either. I couldn't. I wasn't able to do anything more than strip out of my damp and filthy clothes, don some warm pajamas, and gulp down a couple of painkillers with water directly from the bathroom sink.

THINGS did feel different for me the next morning, but not necessarily better. I had a headache the size of Greenland for one thing, and my throat felt scratchy and irritated.

When I opened my eyes to realize exactly where I was, I jumped out of the luxurious Irish linens dressing my bed and wandered into the adjoining sitting room. I went straight to the tea cart Mr. Finnegan had mentioned last night, hoping a hot cup might help soothe my burning throat. I made a mug of my favorite Titanic Blend and poured in a couple of milk pods.

The first sip was heavenly, but it was much too hot to gulp so I took it with me into the bathroom. All I could think about was getting out of this place and to the Belfast airport.

I didn't waste time.

I threw on some clean jeans and a long-sleeved brown shirt that felt soft and comfortable against my sensitive skin. In reality, my body ached all over. I left the muddy stuff from last night where it lay on the floor with little concern. They could throw it all away, I didn't care. Dirty clothes were not my problem right now, getting home was. That and the thought I might be coming down with some kind of vile flu. I was so lost right now, and it wasn't just in the physical sense.

I felt utterly exhausted and weak. The energy expended in self-loathing and embarrassment had taken its toll on me. I downed two more Nurofen to help with the massive pounding going on in my skull combined with the body aches, and gathered up my bag.

What if I had to face Mr. Everley in person again? I couldn't. I just didn't have the strength to deal with that man at the moment.

Or any moment. Ever.

Minutes later I was praying to this fact as I made my way down the grand staircase with my suitcase. I gave it my best Spiderman-stealth-walk and made for the mudroom where everything had gone down last night.

I needed my jacket and remembered he'd hung it up for me dripping wet after our mad dash from the garage through the rain.

Yeah, just before he realized exactly who he'd brought into his home.

He thinks you're a prostitute trying to blackmail him.

A wave of hysteria threatened to overturn me once more and I suddenly felt too overcome to fight it. Just shrugging into my jacket was proving to be a major effort. Thank God it had dried in the night.

I headed for the door, still unsure of how I was going to make it back to my car. The drive up last night from where I'd left it had to have been a couple of miles at least—

"Good morning, Miss Hargreave."

I spun around to find Mr. Finnegan regarding me solemnly, sans smoking jacket. He was dressed in the typical country gentleman uniform of corduroy and tweed.

"You're up very early," he said gently, eyeballing my suitcase. "Will you have some breakfast?" He gestured his hand toward a lighted hallway.

"No, thank you," I said in a pathetically feeble voice. Mr. Finnegan must think I was the biggest freak in the world. "I have to l-leave."

"Are you certain, my dear? I have some fresh scones just out of the oven. A mug of tea? You must be starved by now."

His kindness broke me.

Why couldn't Mr. Finnegan have been the owner of this place and the plethora of artwork I was supposed to inventory? I'd made an express effort to avoid looking at any of the paintings on the walls as I'd come down the stairs. And there had been a shit ton of them to my great dismay. I didn't want to be distracted or waylaid on my course of fleeing, but still, it was really disappointing.

I shook my head and knew I'd started crying again. Between my blubbering, the frustration in realizing I'd never get to see any of the art, feeling like crap, and the injustice of having to beg, I managed to ask my question as I stood there silently weeping. "Mr. Finnegan, will you h-help me get back to my rental car? P-please? I just have to…get away from here—and then I'll be gone—and…Mr. Everley won't ever have to see me again."

I can say he was a gentleman about my emotional outburst. And he didn't try to pry my reasons for going out of me. It looked like he might have rolled his eyes just a bit when I mentioned his employer's name, though. Whether he did or not, Mr. Finnegan calmly led me down to the garage and helped me into the same Range Rover I'd ridden in last night.

The day was rain-free so far, and I hoped it would stay that way until my ass was planted in a seat at thirty thousand feet bound for London Heathrow.

He drove me right to my Volkswagen rental, which hadn't been swept over a cliff in the night, thank God, as if he'd known precisely where it would be parked.

Maybe Mr. Everley had told him all about me, and he already knew about our shameful meeting at the gala, too. At this point, with freedom in my sights, I didn't even care.

Mr. Finnegan did insist upon leading me out to the main road, and pointed me in the direction of Belfast, with clear instructions on how to find my way.

I waved goodbye to him, grateful for his sympathetic help and wishing there was some way for me to repay the kindness he'd shown me—a hot mess of a stranger with major emotional problems who'd upset his boss and dragged him from his warm bed at midnight. He probably wouldn't forget me for a long time. I knew I'd remember him and his Cosmo Topper smoking jacket.

I pondered the disparities in people as I turned onto the highway, relief in the knowledge the airport was less than an hour away, and in a few more hours after that, I'd be back home in *my* warm bed with fuzzy socks on my feet.

I felt as if I could sleep for a year right now. Just so exhausted.

Visions of chicken noodle soup with buttered toast danced in my head. Food would be the first thing I tackled when I got home. I shivered from the chill invading my body and focused my attentions back on the road. I could do this. Every mile was bringing me closer to my goal.

I realized some people, like Mr. Finnegan, were just inherently good.

And others, like Lord Condemnation? *Certifiable asshole* fit him like a leather glove.

Yin and yang.

Chapter 6

"What do you mean she's gone?"

"Some three hours now, I'd say." Finnegan turned his back on me and returned to his task of preparing what looked like a roast of some sort.

"How in the hell was she *able* to leave?"

"I obliged her request that I return her to her hired car. Don't worry, I made sure she arrived safely to the main road and sent her off with directions for Belfast City Airport." He checked his watch absently. "She's probably back to London by now, or close to it."

"Why did you do that, Finnegan? I expected to speak with her this morning about the job." This was certainly an epic cock-up. None of it made any sense. If she came here to find me at home, then why would she leave again so quickly? I didn't think my suggestion last night was that far out of bounds, considering her line of work. The art student part surprised me, true, but maybe scholarly didn't pay enough to suit her tastes. She was a woman who wore silk and lace with ease. Just as she did casual covered in muck.

Once I'd gotten over my initial shock, and cooled down a bit, I'd realized I wanted to keep Maria, or Miss Hargreave, or whatever her name was, around for a while. I wanted to have those green eyes sparking up at me and see her breathing heavily as I crowded her body with mine. I wanted to feel the moment when she decided to submit.

We'd been to that point before, you see, and I was determined to get us there again. I'd realized I'd offended her with my comment about making her come, as soon as I'd said it. She'd smacked me a good one and let me know her limits. I respected that and fully intended to repair my error. Some submissives didn't like things so bluntly put, and I was willing to work out an arrangement that would be completely agreeable to both of us. Or so I had thought. I couldn't deny the more I entertained the idea of her and me having a little something on the side, the more I liked the prospect of getting my artwork catalogued. It might just become my new favorite pastime.

But now she'd just up and left?

This was very displeasing. And Finnegan had helped her to leave.

"I can't believe you helped her to go before I could even have a conversation with her, Finnegan," I said disgustedly. "How in the hell will I get her back here to do the work now?"

He turned slowly and regarded me, his light blue eyes narrowing. "I believe her words to me were, 'I just have to get away from here and Mr. Everley won't ever have to see me again.'"

"What?"

"Yes indeed, she was quite desperate to leave the place, and I feared she would have set off on the road by foot if I'd not helped her. I couldn't have allowed that in her condition," he said firmly, his chin lifting at me in challenge.

"Her condition, Finnegan?" I felt the flicker of unease at my neck. What the bloody fuck did he mean by her *condition*?

"She was distraught, in tears, very upset, and I fear, feverish as well, possibly from being trapped in the wet for so long last night."

Tears? Distraught? Feverish?

"You can't be serious, man," I told him, half hoping I'd heard wrong.

He leveled me the same hairy eyeball that had scared me when I was a boy, and let me have it. "I am deadly serious. When a woman comes to me for help as Miss Hargreave did, then I am at her service, *my Lord.*"

Fuckin' hell.

Finnegan has just used the "my Lord" label on me. I was on his shit list for certain if he was throwing out the dreaded baronial address. The man barely tolerated me as it was and now he'd basically told me to fuck off.

And I feared I'd made a grievous error in how I'd handled the mysterious Miss Hargreave.

I texted her mobile number.

WHY did you just go off? I'd still like for you to do my archival work. Let's discuss. —I Everley

Nothing.

I tried again. **Can we talk about it, please? —I Everley**

And then: **I'll fly you back to Belfast and**

**collect you myself.   No surprises this time.
—I Everley**

No response.

Then I got Langley on the line.

"I can't help you, Ivan. I don't know what in the hell happened up there in Ireland between you two, but she won't help you now for any amount of payment. I believe her words were something along the lines of 'I don't care if he has a basement of lost Vermeers and Van Goghs in crates next to a pile of hidden Nazi gold.'"

"Did she now? I suppose hidden Nazi gold isn't a total impossibility since my grandmother was Russian. Maybe she managed to nick some and stash it. In fact, I'm fairly sure there's a Vermeer in there somewhere, but how in the fuck would she know? She didn't even stay long enough to take a look at anything!" I shook my head in disbelief. "She spoke to you already?"

"She did. She called me from the airport and was not her usual confident self, either. In fact, I've never heard Gabrielle so…upset in the four years I've known her. She told me you didn't want her at your place, that you were very angry when she arrived."

"Yes, well…"

"Were you angry? And if so, why on earth—you practically begged me to send somebody out there."

Yeah, I'd read Gabrielle Hargreave all sorts of wrong. I don't think I could have read her any *more* wrong. *I was so certain though...*

"Ivan?" Langley wasn't going to let go of this.

"Um, yeah. We'd met before you see, and it was...awkward. I suppose I could have handled the situation better. There was a storm and she got lost—all a big misunderstanding."

Langley snorted at me. "Understatement of the year."

"Right, I'll go and see her and apologize then. I want her back here to do the work. Give me Miss Hargreave's address in London and I'll fix this."

"I can't do that. Privacy protection prohibits me from giving out her address. Surely you realize that would be wholly inappropriate."

"But, I definitely want her to do the cataloguing of my art, Langley."

"I'm sorry, Ivan, but I can't help you with her."

"You mean you won't." Langley would find my contribution to his foundation quite lacking in the coming year, but I'd let him worry about it when he missed my cheque.

"Correct," he said firmly.

"Why not?"

He sighed in the line. "Gabrielle told me something quite disturbing, and I find I need to keep some distance between you and the university, in this situation. It's best for all parties involved." He coughed as if preparing himself to say more, and then he continued. "And, Ivan, your recent troubles with…female friends…is no secret. You need to sort your sordid shit out—away and separate from my students."

There it was again. My private life on display for the world to ogle in disgust. Hadn't Miss Hargreave told me I was disgusting right before she cracked me across the face? The idea she thought of me that way really bothered me considering what she does.

"What did she tell you?"

He paused uncomfortably and I could imagine him squirming at his antique desk, probably a lot like mine, as he struggled to lay the uncomfortable truth on me.

"She said you were firmly under the impression she worked for an escort service."

But she does.

"Why on earth would you suggest something so—so coarse, to a student you hoped to make a professional working relationship with?"

Her showing up here took me by surprise and I said the first thoughts that came into my head? And because she is an escort moonlighting at a top-of-the-line private service? Because I want her in both of her professional capacities?

"Ivan?"

"Yeah. I get it, Langley."

"Good, because you can't be terrorizing female students and dragging the university's reputation down into a scandalous goddamn mess—"

I cut the line and simply stared out the window at the sweeping green that went on for miles. So pristinely beautiful. At times I wished there was someone else to share it all with. Besides Finnegan and Marjorie, my groundskeeper.

I mentally kicked myself. What was I thinking? That fantasy idea was dead.

I'd learned long ago that trying to explain myself was utterly pointless most of the time. People usually made up their minds in advance. Didn't really matter what Langley thought of me, anyway. I knew the truth about Gabrielle Hargreave and I'd find her again. There were ways to make that happen, and I had the resources.

The storm had passed through during the night leaving scattered clouds and mild temperatures behind. It appeared the day might stay dry, and I was grateful her drive down to Belfast was made safer with no dangerous weather messing up the roads. At least there was that.

I texted my dad just before the flight attendant called for all cellular devices to be switched to airplane mode. **The job in Ireland didn't work out. Arriving Heathrow @ 11:30 on BA 1423. Can you pick me up? Don't worry. xo -Gaby**

The drive to Belfast, turning in the rental car, waiting in line to buy a ticket, and then the ordeal of getting my equipment through as checked baggage had pretty much wiped me out. I touched my forehead with the back of my hand in an attempt to feel if I was hot. I couldn't really tell for sure, but maybe I had a fever. I knew I felt like shit, and that was plenty, fever or not. If I was indeed getting sick it sure explained a lot about my emotional state of the past sixteen hours. The crying and weeping was so out of character for me.

Poor Mr. Finnegan. *No, thank God for Mr. Finnegan.*

Had Mr. Everley inquired about me after I'd gone? He'd probably felt relieved to know his private sanctuary was back to being private again. The man really thought I was a prostitute. Total insanity. *Well, not really, considering what you allowed him to do to you on the night of the gala.* I shivered in shame, pretty sure I made an audible groan, because the guy seated next to me was all eyes and instant attention. I ignored him and turned away toward the window.

Professor Langley sure hadn't expected the "Mr. Everley thinks I'm working for an escort service" announcement to come out of my mouth. But then, neither had I. Regardless, it got me off the hook of having to stay there and do the job. The whole nightmare was over, and I was free now, but still…I shuddered in mortification at the thought of what Mr. Everley had said about wanting to fuck me…and for how I'd slapped him. I had never behaved like I had with him with other men, both on the night of the gala, and last night at his estate. He affected me strangely for sure, and I said and did things that shocked even me.

It was just so damned awful, the whole thing. And I was certain I was coming down with something evil.

I rested my feverish head against the cool window and continued to ignore my early-balding, over-cologned seat-mate who kept trying desperately to get my attention, and didn't seem to take the hint I wasn't interested in being on the receiving end of his, can-I-buy-you-a-drink?, come on. Ugh.

I closed my eyes and slept.

MY dad wasn't there to pick me up. He sent Desmond to do it.

Just seeing a friendly face nearly propelled me back into tearful territory.

"Jesus Christ, you're hot, Gaby," he said after a kiss to my cheek.

I frowned at him and felt my eyes get watery.

"I—I mean you feel hot." Des looked me over good, his warm brown eyes darting. "Are you all right? You don't look your usual self," he said more gently.

Was that a nice way to tell me I looked like shit? I sure felt like a giant pile of it, and I must've looked the same. I forced a smile, gulped back my tears, and thought maybe I should give Desmond Thorne a chance.

The man was always nice to me, and despite his serious persona, he was dependable. No crazy irrationality coming out of him. He was also gorgeous, with a lean body trimmed in muscles I knew would be spectacular if I ever saw it sans the designer suit. Des was always wearing a suit, so I'd never had the privilege. Didn't mean the spectacular body wasn't rippling under the silk threads. Also didn't mean I couldn't have the privilege if I wanted. I could. In a heartbeat. All I had to do was let him know I wanted to.

But did I? This was the burning question.

Along with my burning body temp.

"I know. I think I have a fever." I held a hand up. "You probably shouldn't get too close, Des. I'd hate to give you whatever it is that's infected me."

"Don't you worry about me, Gaby. I am never ill." He reached for my baggage trolley and took over pushing it for me. "Your flat then, I'm guessing?"

I nodded gratefully. "Yeah. I just want to get into my bed and sleep for a long time."

"Of course."

We talked in the car on the way into the city. I told him how I'd gotten lost in the storm and had to wait in the dark for three hours until Mr. Everley finally decided to answer his messages. I explained how he was angry when I'd arrived and thought I was somebody named Maria, and felt his privacy had been compromised. I left out the part about how we'd hooked up at the National Gallery. Just the remembrance right now gave me a shiver. I shared that Mr. Everley might be a jerk, but his servant, Mr. Finnegan, was most certainly not. How he had been kind and showed me to my room, and then helped me this morning to make it back to my rental car.

"It sounds like this Everley's a crazy bastard, and I'm glad you're not taking his job. And your dad will be glad, too."

"I know he will. Dad doesn't trust most people."

Des cracked a tiny smile and raised an eyebrow at me.

"I know he trusts you," I said absently as I switched my phone off airplane mode, and waited for it to update.

There were three alerts. Texts. All from *him*.

I read them and couldn't believe my eyes.

"Oh—my—God. The lunatic is asking me to come back there and accept the job."

"What is he saying?" Des asked.

I read the texts out loud to him.

"Why is he fucking you about like this? He's angry you've come to his estate and wants you gone, and then when you've left the job, he begs you to stay? You're right, he is a lunatic plonker."

I said nothing. I couldn't tell anyone I'd had a sexual encounter with the man. Instead I decided right then and there to put the nightmare experience of Mr. Everley behind me for good. I'd made a terrible lapse in judgment the night of the gala in a moment of weakness, and I had paid for my sin. I needed to put the whole hideous mess behind me and move on.

By the time we got to my flat, I could hardly stand on my feet without wavering. Desmond helped me up all five flights of stairs, his strong arms practically carrying me.

I did manage to dredge up enough energy to change into some yoga pants and a T-shirt, and to crawl into my bed while he went back down to get my bags.

Des was such a good person, I thought, as I settled under the covers and let my eyes close. I should maybe thank him by inviting him over to Dad's place for a home cooked dinner. Yeah, I might just do that once I was feeling better...

ENOUGH of this silent-treatment bullshit. I phoned her.

Except it wasn't her. Some chap answered.

"I'd like to speak to Gabrielle Hargreave," I said.

"And who's asking?" So, I'd gotten the correct number for her at least, but the voice on the other end of the line was hostile, so I figured there was nothing to lose.

"My name is Everley and I want to speak with her about a job she was hired to do at my home."

"Well, she doesn't want your blasted job, and she's not coming back there ever, you fuckin' prick."

"Who is this speaking?"

"Someone who cares about her. Someone who cares that she's ill with a fever right now, and worn out from the crazy shit you bloody well know you put her through. Who abandons a woman out in a storm for hours and then tells her she needs to leave as soon as she arrives? Who does that and then bothers her with messages to come back there?"

"I've made a mistake and I need to speak with her. Can you tell her to ring me?"

"I doubt it, but what I *can* tell you is that you're going to fuck right off."

Then the line went dead.

I'd bet money he wasn't her man because he'd have said so if he was. She'd never corrected me when I'd addressed her as "Miss" either. Whoever that was who'd answered her mobile was somebody close, yes, but he wasn't her husband and he wasn't her boyfriend.

He said she was ill, and that part didn't sit well with me.

I felt badly about her being frightened and

feeling unwell as she tried to find the house in the storm. I felt even worse about how I'd blown up at her when I saw her in the light and got a good look. What were the odds of that happening? She was such a goddamn mystery, no doubt about it. Was she an escort sent to dig up more sordid dirt on me, or had that part been all a misunderstanding as well? She claimed over and over she wasn't working for any escort service. Langley was appalled at the suggestion. Finnegan had labeled me a tyrant, as had her unnamed telephone champion. Was I way off the mark with Gabrielle Hargreave?

I couldn't stop thinking about the way she'd been in that closet with me at the National Gallery, though. It played and replayed over and over in my head. My body remembered all too well how she felt deliciously melted in my arms, submissive and content after I'd made her come. How she'd wanted everything we did together in those too-short minutes. That encounter had been all about the sex. Mad, bang-on, dirty sex. I wanted to have her like that again. I wanted to believe she was just a grad student sent to do some important work, who just happened to have some incredible chemistry with me. I could still remember how she tasted, sweet and exotic, and how she let me have my way.

Tantalizing infuriating woman.

Priceless

I went outside for my daily therapy in hopes of figuring it all out.

As I shot arrow after arrow into the targets, I thought about what had happened with her, and wondered if I would ever see her again. Or if I did manage to find her, would she ever allow me to apologize and make it up to her? It bothered me very much she was ill and had to travel on her own while feeling that way. I was sorry for upsetting her to the point of tears and driving her away. I needed to see her again so I could attempt to figure out where things had turned so horribly wrong. How had I read her so inaccurately?

I'd get my chance eventually. Despite my lot in life, I was genuinely optimistic about most things. And confident. It was just part of how I'd been made, and I knew how to fight for the win. I'd done it plenty of times, and under extreme pressures most people would never understand.

I did have her number. Gabrielle Hargreave would have to answer her own mobile phone sooner or later. And I would be on the other end of the line when she did.

Chapter 7

London
15th August

"Are you one hundred percent recovered, my lovely?"

"Getting there. You'll be pleased to know I am not carrying any pathogens capable of sending you to bed for a week straight. I'm still on antibiotics for another ten days."

"Depends on who's in the bed with me, love." Ben loved to tease with innuendo.

I laughed at him. "Well, trust me, you wouldn't

be thinking about sex for the next century if you felt like I did this past week. Strep throat is killer on the libido, Benny."

"The main cause of strep throat is stress, you know. If you had more sex, you wouldn't be so stressed."

"Oh please. You are not feeding me that old line to go have random sex with some strange penis to avoid getting sick."

He cocked a brow at me and smirked. "Do I ever seem stressed to you?"

I sighed and shook my head. "No. You never are."

Ben bowed gallantly next to a rack of vintage gowns. "I rest my case, darling."

"Easy for you to say," I muttered as I flicked through some possibilities for a dress as maid-of-honor at Brynne and Ethan's wedding. "You're a guy and have no morals."

He ignored my insult. Probably because he knew it was legitimate fact.

"What about the copper? Declan? He'd step up and help you work off some stress I'm sure." Ben pulled out a strapless vintage Carolina Herrera in burgundy lace and set it aside for me to try on. "And he's fit."

"Desmond. I know he would, but it doesn't feel

right to me for some reason." And it didn't. Something was holding me back because if I'd ever been given signals from Des, they had come in the past week. I might have been out of it, but I wasn't dead.

After I'd arisen from my initial coma, I'd found some soup in the fridge with instructions to heat it up and eat it. He also made sure my dad was filled in on my health status. I had ended up with strep throat and a visit to a walk-in urgent care centre at Lord Guildford Hospital to get some serious meds to kill the raging infection. The pain had been severe, and I'd done nothing but sleep and drink soothing broths and teas for days. Dad had insisted I stay at his house to recuperate because he didn't want me all alone at my flat, now that Brynne had moved out. I seriously wondered what would have happened to me if Des hadn't picked me up from the airport and clued in on how sick I really was. Nobody would have known.

"What doesn't feel right about having some mutually agreed upon pleasure? Don't overthink things with him. Just give it up and enjoy yourself. I swear you'll feel better, and I can hear all the deets on how he does." He held up a pink frothy mess trimmed in ostrich feathers and studied it.

"You're horrible, and so is that feather dress." I

shook my head slowly at both of them. "No, I can't do that to Desmond. I'd be using him and he deserves much better." I plucked chiffon in pale lavender-grey off the rack that looked promising.

"What am I going to do with you, lady? You need a man to satisfy your needs."

"No, I really don't."

"Yes, you very much do," he said stubbornly, gathering up the gowns we'd chosen and gesturing toward the dressing room with a jerk of his head. "Now get in there and start trying frocks."

I shut the door on him and shimmied out of my clothes. Time was running out to get the dress thing sorted out. My illness had put me way behind schedule. Brynne was so non-stress about it though. She'd given us free reign on the bridesmaid dresses and said she didn't care if they were even remotely the same. I was trying to keep it in the purple/lavender realm and so were the others. Brynne asked me to be her maid-of-honor and Elaina and Hannah to be bridesmaids. Hannah was Ethan's older sister, and it was at her country mansion where their wedding would take place. A garden wedding meant a more casual dress was okay, but at the same time, it was going to be a very posh event with lots of celebrities attending. I wanted my gown to be right.

"Maybe you'll meet someone at the wedding

who can take care of your little problem," Ben chatted at me through the dressing room door.

"I doubt it, and I don't have a problem, Benny." I glared up at him from behind the dressing room door. "Humans can live productive lives without frequent sex, you know."

He vetoed the lilac crushed velvet with a sharp shake of his head as soon as I stepped out. "Maybe they can be productive, but not very happy. I want you to be happy," he said seriously.

I mouthed "thank you" and an air kiss and went back into the dressing room. I tried the Carolina Herrera next. "This isn't gonna work." I stepped out to show him. "I'm not doing this weird lace. It looks like it's been made from a chenille bedspread."

"Agree," Ben said. "Who will be your partner at the wedding?"

"Umm, I know Ethan asked his cousin to be best man. Brynne told me his name before but I don't remember. He does some kind of sport. I think it might be fencing or lacrosse maybe? I know she said he was involved with announcing some of the events for the Olympics." I smoothed the skirt of the lavender floaty chiffon, turning back and forth to make the skirt move. "It was right around the time her dad passed away, so…" I trailed off on that sobering thought. Ben and I had been with Brynne when the call came through that her father had drowned in his swimming pool. I don't think I would ever forget the horribleness of that day. The poor girl had been through some dark and terrible times leading up to this wedding. She had tearfully asked Ben to give her away, which had touched him deeply. We all just wanted some peace and happiness for her and Ethan. They surely deserved some.

"I think we might have a winner," I announced as I stepped out. "What is your opinion, Mr. Clarkson?"

He swept his eyes up and down me with a critical eye. He circled his finger for me to turn for him. Ben was all seriousness when it came to clothing. I knew he was evaluating how to accessorize me and fix my hair. He was brutally honest and would tell me if it was a good choice. Or not. Our relationship had always been an honest one, which was why he could talk to me about personal things off limits with most people.

"Do you feel pretty in that one then?"

"I do. Yes. Thank you for helping me." I pushed up on my toes to kiss him on the cheek. "What would I do without you to choose my clothes?"

He snickered down at me with a smug look on

his handsome face. "I have absolutely no idea, my darling."

Somerset
22ⁿᵈ August

LAKE Leticia was just large enough for my Cessna T206. A floatplane required only two hundred metres to safely manoeuver a landing, but five hundred were needed to take off again. The private lake on my cousin's estate made my trip over from Donadea quick and painless. No driving at all, just a pleasant trip across the Irish Sea. Lake to lake it only took me an hour.

The biggest hassle was anchoring and tying her down so when I wanted to take off three days from now, she wasn't drifting about in the *middle* of Lake Leticia. The tiny loading dock for rowboats served just fine for Nelly's purposes. I pulled her up alongside, dropped anchor, and did up the ropes.

Colin and Jordan greeted me on the dock with typical boyish enthusiasm and insisted on carrying my bags. Hannah and Freddy were raising some wonderful kids and made it look so easy when it wasn't. As I was well aware.

That's because nothing good and worthwhile is ever easy.

I'd learned that lesson the hard way.

"Did you bring your bow, Ivan? The one you used in 2008 when you won the gold medal? Did you bring your medals with you? Will you let us shoot it again?" They pelted me with questions.

"Gentleman, what do you think are in those cases you're carrying?" I held up my leather bag. "I've got you lads hauling the important stuff. This is just my clothes."

"You wouldn't let us carry the cases if you didn't trust us, right?" Jordan asked.

"That's right." I buzzed the top of his hair with my hand and let them lead me up to the house, their chatter dominating the conversation the entire way.

It felt really good to be with them again.

"I'M so glad you came up this afternoon before things really turn nutter around here. We actually might be able to have a visit for once," Hannah told me over the family table. "We don't see you enough, Ivan."

"Me too," I answered quietly. "Where else can I get a gourmet meal and eat with a princess?" I winked at Zara, Hannah and Freddy's youngest, who sat glued to my side enjoying her dish of strawberry ice cream.

"Mummy said Prince Harry is coming to Uncle Ethan's wedding. He's a real prince," she informed me with a grin and big blue eyes that would charm the ever living hell out of many a bloke, princes included, in another decade or so. Probably less time than that. She was only five and already breaking hearts everywhere. I was still amused by Ethan's telling of how Zara had been the one to spill the beans that "Auntie Brynne was preggers whether she likes it or not."

Out of the mouths of babes.

The surprise pregnancy turned out to have been the best thing for them, though. I'd never seen Ethan so grounded as he'd become since finding Brynne and discovering they were going to have a child. Brynne had utterly transformed him. Despite their troubles, and there had been some nasty ones, they were making a go of things together, and I had no doubts they'd do splendidly. After all, when you love a person, and they love you back, just about any storm can be weathered.

But they have to love you back or it doesn't work...

"Prince Harry is far too old for you, young lady." I stuck my spoon into Zara's bowl and stole a bit of her ice cream while making a show of it with some sneaky sound effects.

She giggled at me again and held her bowl up closer so I could have some more if I liked, the generous offer to share with me so sweetly and freely given. Children had this quality when they were young, but it went away as the years passed, and the learning of the harsh lessons of life. It happened to all of us, and it would happen to Zara someday. We learned to protect our hearts a little more with each time something came along to hurt it.

Sad, but true.

Growing up an only child, I'd depended on my Blackstone cousins a great deal more than they did me, because they'd had each other after our mothers died together in the same car crash.

They'd also had a father that paid attention to them.

Hannah, being older, had pretty much slipped into the big-sister role with me along with Ethan. I loved her for it, and there wasn't anything I wouldn't do for her, or her family. Her husband Fred, or Dr. Greymont as he was known amongst the locals, was a country doctor along with helping her to run Hallborough House as an upscale bed and breakfast hotel. I admired them so much. Their family, the life they had created, the people they were. They had everything I didn't have, and yet they loved me in spite of my sordid cock-up of an existence. There was never any judgment or censure with Hannah and Freddy. I was in tight with them. Damn, if that didn't feel fucking wonderful I couldn't say what did.

Ethan and Brynne were going to have what Hannah and Freddy had together.

The purpose for my visit here was to get my cousin ball-n-chained, after all. The rehearsal was tomorrow and the wedding the following day, so this weekend was all about my family and supporting something good and blessed for once.

Being asked by Ethan to stand up for him as his best man was an honour and a privilege for me. It created feelings I rarely felt, and had trouble processing whenever I did. I'd have to give it my best shot, of course. This was the universal understanding amongst Hannah, Ethan, and me that went back as far as we did together. If any of us ever needed the other, or help of any kind, we would be there. No questions asked and no problem.

The sound of a car horn blasted obnoxiously from out the front, interrupting my thoughts, and announcing the beginnings of an invasion that would only grow to epic proportions in the next days as the hoards made their way to the celebrity wedding of the summer.

"Now that sounds to me as if the bride and

groom have finally arrived," Fred announced his prediction.

The three kids jumped up from the table eager and bouncing to get outside to greet Ethan and Brynne.

"Yep, I'd say that was the starting buzzer, all right. Game on now," I told them, "the die is cast, my dears, and you don't have a choice about hosting this do anymore."

Hannah laughed at my comment and snuck her arm around my waist as we followed the kids outside.

It was really happening.

Ethan Blackstone was gettin' shackled.

EVENT planners deserved the Nobel Prize. My cousin surely did, anyway.

Good, fucking lord I don't know how Hannah managed to pull this soiree together and not lob anyone's head off. The furor going on around me made me consider just getting the hell out of the way. Would anyone notice if I snuck off in Nelly and flew her back to Donadea?

Come tomorrow afternoon somebody might notice. I'd better just man up and try to make myself useful.

Ethan and Brynne were busy with settling in her mum and step-dad, Hannah was directing at least three different crews working on separate things: organizing the new house for the wedding night, the raising of a tent city in the garden, and other crap that overwhelmed me. Fred had been called to hospital, and I'd kept the kids busy all morning with target practice. Uncle Jonathan had taken them to the cinema about an hour ago, and I was now with nothing to do but arse about.

I texted Hannah. **Put me to work, lady.**

She hit me right back. **God I luv u. I need u to p/u Brynne's people @ Taunton Sta. and bring here. Take my car. Keys on pantry hook. 3 guests - Ben, Gaby & Mum. Ben will stand in 4 her dad and Gaby is MoH. Thank u!!!**

Now this was a job I could manage without a cock-up. Collect wedding party guests from the railway and bring them here. **I can do that. xo**

I was guessing that MoH meant maid-of-honour. So this would be my partner I was meeting. And I remembered E telling me about Brynne's photographer friend she'd asked to give her away at the ceremony. Sweet girl had recently lost her father in an accident Ethan wasn't convinced had been an accident. Heinously tragic situation with no good outcome.

Priceless

Yeah, the world was full of insane fuckers for sure. I certainly had no trouble attracting them either.

Chapter 8

Ben read the message from Ethan's sister to us out loud from his phone, "My cousin is on his way to you now and will bring you up to Hallborough. Look for the tall deadly handsome one. You can't miss him. LOL. See you soon. Hannah."

One look at his wide, suggestive eyes paired with the leering grin and I knew exactly what Benny was thinking.

I shook my head at him and rolled my eyes right

back. "Filan, your son thinks his mission in life is to find me a man. Can you make him stop?" I pleaded to Ben's mom.

"Oh, my darling, Gabriellen, I think not. You are too beautiful to be without a man holding you happy in his arms at night."

I threw up my hands in frustration and raised my eyes heavenward. "I see where he gets it now."

Filan Clarkson loved her son so very much, but she also loved to mother his friends. She always called me Gabriellen no matter how many times I told her there was no "n" on the end of my name. I'd given up correcting her a long time ago, and I didn't really even care at this point. She was a stunning woman, a former fashion model who'd made a life for herself in London after fleeing her native Somalia. It was easy to see where Ben got his drive to succeed, as well as his looks. She loved to cook big Sunday meals and invite everyone over to eat. And having someone mother you when your own was gone wasn't a terribly bad thing after all. I turned away and left them there snickering behind my back while I went to find the loo.

I checked myself in the station bathroom and saw how pale I looked. The strep throat had definitely taken a toll on my body. I'd lost weight and didn't at all look my best, but there was nothing I could do about it. I pinched my cheeks and shook a hand through my hair to fluff it out before I stopped myself and asked why in the hell it even mattered. I wasn't the bride. Nobody would be looking at me.

It was time for me to take a pill anyway. My antibiotics still had two days to go before I finished. The doctor had been strict about taking the pills on time, and until the last one was gone, or I could have a reoccurrence. Nope. Not happening. One bout of strep was more than enough and I never wanted to experience that kind of pain or sickness again.

I headed to the concession area inside the station and bought a bottle of Vitamin Water Orange-Orange. My favorite. I swallowed my horse pill and went back outside to where I'd left Ben and Filan.

I could see that our "ride" had found them while I was off. I guessed he must be the cousin, because he shook Ben's hand before politely greeting Filan. He was tall like Hannah had mentioned, but I couldn't tell about the "deadly handsome" part because his back was facing me as I walked toward them. His ass looked good in the jeans he was wearing. Um, yeah.

Ben saw me coming and held out his hand, urging me over. "Gaby, this is Ivan, Ethan's cousin and best man for the wedding."

I put a smile on my face in preparation of

meeting my partner for the weekend. No need to be unfriendly. Hopefully he was as nice as he looked…

He started to turn toward me.

"Ivan, meet Gaby. Brynne's maid-of-honour to your best man."

I noticed the hair first. He had the kind of hair you remembered.

Then the shape of his chiseled jaw as he turned his head.

Finally, it was the eyes that verified things for me. Those arresting green eyes of his latched onto mine for the third time in my life.

No, it cannot be him. Ivan. Ivanhoe.

This just couldn't be right.

But it was him. And Ivan *was* his name. A wave of desperation hit me as I remembered him telling me his full name. He'd introduced himself properly when we'd both made a second attempt at introductions before everything blew up. He'd turned to me in the front seat of his car and said, "Gabrielle Hargreave, it's a pleasure to meet you. Ivan Everley, inheritor of all this…and of course, shuttle driver for lost American art students."

Everything clicked into place in those long seconds as I froze in step on the train station platform. It all made sense now. Who he was. Why he'd attended the Mallerton Gala that night. How he had connections to Paul Langley and the university.

Brynne had wanted me to meet him. She'd tried to introduce us before her life was turned upside down with a surprise pregnancy and then the death of her father.

Why didn't I figure this out before?

Ivan Everley was Ethan's cousin who owned the houseful of paintings...

And I was so dreadfully screwed right now.

I lifted my chin and stood there, waiting to be called out by him, my proverbial neck stretched out on the chopping block ready for his axe.

But it didn't happen like that.

No, instead he flashed me a smile that hit me right in the chest, and extended his hand.

"Gaby. So nice to finally meet you. E's been telling me about you for weeks."

I stared down at his hand and then looked up at his face again.

Smooth and calm, he kept with the devastating smile, hand still reaching out, waiting for me to take hold.

He's pretending we've never met before.

My whole body seized into a state of paralysis.

Thank God he's pretending we've never met before.

I just stood there like a mute, relief coursing through me in a torrent.

Ben cleared his throat and asked, "Are you all right, luv?"

Filan laid the back of her hand on my forehead to check if I was feverish and inquired, "Gabriellen?"

"You look like you've just seen a ghost, Gaby," Ivan said softly, tilting his head at me in question. "I hope I haven't frightened you." His deep green eyes sparked in amusement, the color even more stunning in the full light of day.

"Ivan, h-h-hello," I breathed, "n-no, you h-haven't." I put my hand into his and felt the heat of his skin as he shook it. More gibberish came out of my mouth, but I couldn't say what exactly as I was having trouble controlling my breathing to speak any words at all.

Then he winked at me. And stroked his index finger along my palm as he pulled away.

A squeaky moan escaped my throat.

I could feel each of their eyes on me, probably wondering what in the hell kind of affliction had suddenly overtaken me. Ivan looked positively gleeful. *Ass.*

Filan broke the tension. "Our Gabriellen has been ill you know, Mr. Everley, and I think the train has exhausted her and she needs to rest in bed before rehearsal tonight."

He gave an elegant bow of his head. "Of course

she does, Mrs. Clarkson." Then he moved beside me and pressed his hand to my back. "It sounds to me like you're being put to bed, whether you need it or not, *Gaby*," he said teasingly, before steering us toward a silver-blue Range Rover. He opened the front passenger side door for me and gestured with his other hand. "In you go."

"Thanks," I managed, unable to do anything other than follow his instructions.

While Ben loaded our luggage, Ivan settled me in and helped me with my seatbelt, the delicious scent of him invading my senses and bringing back memories I couldn't afford to have banging around in my head again.

As he pulled back I swear he inhaled a breath and I felt the tips of his hair brush over the side of my jaw, making a tingle slide down my spine.

No way.

How in the hell would I survive the next three days with him?

I didn't say anything as Ben and Filan chatted with Ivan on the drive. I observed and assessed, too shocked to join in. I needed a bit of time with this whole thing.

Ivan's hands were beautiful just like the rest of him. There was an unusual tattoo on his right ring finger that I got quick glimpses of when we'd stop at a light and he'd release the hold on the steering wheel. From what I could tell, it looked like a heraldic crest. Then I remembered he was aristocracy. He'd corrected me when I'd said he was an earl and told me he was only a "lowly baron." He didn't seem to be worried about our meeting in the slightest. In fact, he looked supremely pleased with himself, *and* very amused by our situation.

The cocky grin on his face stayed there for the entire drive up to Hallborough.

Motherfucker-asshole-shithead-bastard.

"YEAH, well, Elaina's friend from France will be maid-of-honour now, and I need to add another groomsman to even out the couples. I know the wedding's only six weeks out, but will you do it, mate?"

McManus was a good mate. I'd met him through E of course, but we'd logged some serious hours together over the years and I knew he was asking because he counted me as the same. I was happy for him and Elaina. Happy for Ethan and Brynne. Happy for my people who'd managed to find the one they couldn't dream of living without.

If I was totally honest I could accept that the feeling had never been there for me. Not even with...*her.*

We all know she certainly didn't feel it for me—

Neil interrupted my morose thoughts about my ex with something far more intriguing. "You've met Gaby, yeah? Elaina said she'd pair the two of you up together at ours. She's beautiful, intelligent, and a complete darling. I'm sure the two of you will get on brilliantly."

My head snapped up to meet his suggestive grin and my brain switched the fuck on.

"Right," I said smoothly. "Gaby is lovely, I agree. I've only just met her a while ago when Hannah sent me down to the station to bring them up to the house." It appeared that we were both lying about having met before. I had no problem with pretending if she didn't.

"So, can I tell Elaina you're on for it?" Neil asked hopefully.

"How can I say no to you, you romantic sod? I'd be honoured to stand up for you while you shackle yourself to your beloved."

Neil clapped me on the back and thanked me enthusiastically while I did a silent fist pump in the air. Score one for me. He raised his Guinness to my

Bombay & Schweppes in salute.

Fate could be a beautiful thing, I realized as I tapped drinks with my friend.

I'd found her again just like I'd hoped, even if I don't think I could've been more surprised by the circumstances. My mysterious obsession was connected directly to my own flesh and blood. E and Brynne had both talked about Gaby to me. Both had expressed how much they wanted us to meet on more than one occasion.

Well we did, actually. And all on our own. And definitely not in the way you'd expect.

What were the odds?

I had her in my sights for the weekend, and would again in six weeks when Neil and Elaina tied the knot in Scotland. Oh, this was priceless.

Gaby. I rolled the name around in my mouth silently.

I liked the sound of Gabrielle more. It fit her exquisite beauty to perfection.

She was Gabrielle to me. Especially since I now understood that "Maria" was just a specter from a night when confusion and mistaken identity had ruled. I now had the real name for the real woman, and for some reason, it felt fucking victorious.

But I don't think she was too happy about seeing me. She'd been so quiet on the drive up to the house, sitting stiffly in the seat within inches of me, breathing in soft deep pulls that made me want to feel them against my skin. Make that *her* skin on *my* skin. Naked.

Gabrielle Hargreave pushed all of my buttons, and in just the right way. I was pretty sure I pushed hers as well, even if she wasn't ready to admit it just yet.

I would let her absorb the blow of finding out exactly how we fit into the other's world for the moment. This whole thing *was* a shock, I'd agree with her on that point. But now with our little freakout behind us, there was nothing for it but to go forward. I'd get her alone later on and tell her what I needed to say. And she would listen to me this time.

She didn't have another option.

I grinned at Neil as he went off to get us another round of drinks. Gabrielle was firmly in my world now, and there would be no escape for her.

Not during the next three days at least.

HER arse. The skirt clinging to it. Her skirt was tight and black with colourful flowers wrapping around front to back. Looked *very* nice paired with her long legs and black heels. *I've had my fingers up in*

between those lovely legs…

Yeah…I wished I was that skirt right now. I know she saw me pegging her the moment she came into the garden for rehearsal with the others, too, but she ignored me and turned away to talk to Brynne's mum.

Which was how I got the chance to study her spectacular arse again. I hadn't forgotten how nice it looked in jeans, either, from the night when she showed up to Donadea.

I'd take the view and bide my time. I can play nice when the occasion calls. Expert at faking, remember?

Gabrielle was expert at pretending we were strangers. So fucking sexy watching her play aloof. She'd been doing it steadily since our meeting at the station. Once we arrived at the house, there had been no chance to get her alone because guests were arriving in droves by that point. Brynne and Elaina had swept her away somewhere and I was left doing duty keeping my cousin from chain-smoking himself into an early grave with those goddamn Djarum Black coffin nails he was addicted to.

Neil and I decided that hiding his stash was for his own good. Tough love and all that crap.

"I need a fucking cigarette," E complained beside me as the vicar droned on about the particulars.

I stared at him, pretty bloody sure he'd just read my mind, the clever bastard. "No time for that now, brother. Pay attention to the man or you won't know what to do tomorrow afternoon." I nodded toward the end of the path where his girl was waiting to walk down for this practice run-through.

His expression brightened as soon as Brynne came into view with Clarkson leading her. Christ, talk about a man so head-over-heels he didn't know if he was coming or going. E still surprised me very much. I was happy for him, of course, but to see him like this was something that needed a little getting used to.

Clarkson was an interesting fellow as well. I knew he was a photographer and had been the one to take Brynne's nude portraits. Well, the one E had purchased the night he'd met Brynne in London. Gabrielle and Clarkson seemed very close and I wondered what the story was there. He was gay, and Gabrielle, as far as I could tell, wasn't. Had Clarkson taken pictures of Gabrielle as well? Flesh shots? I wanted them if *they* existed. There were so many unanswered questions I wanted to ask…

"Now the couples will exit behind the bride and groom with the best man leading our maid-of-honour," the vicar announced.

Showtime.

I smiled at Gabrielle as I met her in the middle, holding out my arm.

She didn't want to take my arm, but then she was without options. The whole effect got my cock twitching as I pulled her into my side and walked us out, not missing the fact that she fit perfectly against me.

"Finally," I said, looking down at her.

"I'm sorry, did you say something?" She kept her eyes straight ahead.

"We need to have an adult conversation, Gabrielle, don't you think?"

"Oh, you want to act like an adult now?"

"Mmm hmm, I do."

"So you must've given up on the idea that I'm Maria-the-Escort you paid to service you. That had to have been a devastating *blow* for you, Ivan."

I caught her sexual innuendo and imagined exactly what she could blow.

"It does seem the logical conclusion. Didn't Sherlock Holmes say something like once you eliminate the impossible—"

"—whatever remains, no matter how improbable, must be the truth." She finally looked up at me as she finished the quote.

God, she was lovely, and I so wanted her in my

137

bed all fiery and wild as I took control of her pleasure again. Even if she wasn't ready for that yet, I still fantasized.

"Conan-Doyle fan?"

"I know my Sherlock Holmes. I read the whole volume in college. Checked it out at the library and dragged it to the beach with me all summer."

"And where was this?"

"University of California at Santa Barbara."

"A very beautiful coastline you have in your home state."

She didn't respond, and I knew exactly what she was doing. Trying to reassert control over our conversation by withholding her participation, and regretting she'd told me anything at all. I knew all the tricks.

I led her to our dinner table and seated her, resting my hands on her shoulders and holding them there for a moment longer than necessary. I couldn't help it. I had to have my hands on her again.

She took her seat stiffly, probably trying to figure how she could get away from me, but I wasn't having it. She was mine for the course of this meal and hopefully afterward. One small victory at a time.

"Eat your soup, Miss Hargreave, you're not going anywhere for a while." I winked.

She glared at me and then took a bite of what I

guessed was a corn bisque of some sort. Watching her take a spoonful and then swallow, her elegant neck moving in reflex was quite the show. I waited for her to hit me back with something cheeky but she stayed quiet and took another spoonful of the soup.

"I phoned you and sent texts," I said softly.

She kept her head down. "I wouldn't know because I've been off the grid leading up to this wedding."

"I was very sorry to hear you were ill."

Finally she gave me her gorgeous face again. The words were sarcastic as hell, but at least I got to look at her.

"Yeah. I had to go to Ireland for this horrible job. Worst assignment ever. I got lost in a frightening storm and thought I was going to die. And then…once I made it to shelter, my boss was an asshole of such epic proportions my body just succumbed, I guess. He couldn't decide if he wanted me to stay or go, and I think, was suffering from a case of insanity." She pretended to ponder by tilting her head and nodding. "Yeah, completely insane I'm sure of it, poor man." Another spoonful of soup. "I had to drive away from his estate with a raging fever the next morning, but I escaped with the help of a kindly servant." She stonefaced me. "Mr. Finnegan was his name and I'll never forget him. The insane boss? I'm trying to forget I ever *met* him." She took a healthy swig of her drink and sighed dramatically. "It's been really difficult for me because he keeps showing up in the same places as me."

Ouch.

I shook my head. "I want you to know I feel really badly about that. About all of it. The part about making you wait in the storm, being an arsehole, about scaring you, and most of all, for not being the one to take care of you when you were ill."

"Why?"

"I'm not a monster, Gabrielle. I hate that you felt the need to flee my home, and me, when you had a fever. You could have crashed your car and been killed on the road." If she only knew how much the thought of anyone being hurt as a result of my actions really bothered me.

She lowered her voice. "No, I mean why didn't you let on to the others that we'd met before?"

"It seemed the gentlemanly thing to do."

"Ha," she scoffed. "You, a gentleman? That's a stretch, don't you think?"

"Probably, but for you I'll make an exception."

She frowned, biting one corner of her luscious bottom lip. I wanted to lick it.

"I think you're beautiful."

Her gaze flickered over my face and I think, my

hair, but she didn't say anything. I didn't have to wonder if she liked what she saw. I could tell she did.

"I tried to apologize to you by phone. Several times. If Langley had given me your address it would have been in person."

"I told you I was sick," she snapped.

"Yes...and now you're better."

She glared at me and drank more of her blueberry mojito. I wanted to stick my tongue in her mouth and taste the lingering flavors.

"And there's something else you need to know," I told her.

"You flunked out of Being a Human 101 but aced Assholery III?" The sarcastic sneer on her lovely lips was sexy as fuck and I couldn't help laughing at the witty comeback.

"You're coming back with me to Donadea after this wedding, Miss Hargreave."

"It'll never happen, Mr. Ever—" She lost the rest of my name in mid-speech and swallowed hard.

My cock liked that. A lot.

"I love to hear you address me as *mister*," I said, "and we'll work all that out later, lovely thing."

My inner Dom was switched on instantly and ready to go off somewhere private with the submissive goddess in Miss Hargreave and take things to the next level.

But she wasn't ready yet, and I had more work to do first.

She looked like she was about to bolt.

"There isn't going to be a *later.*"

"Oh, there will be, I promise you," I said, looking right at her mouth. "I can see you're just as affected, sweetheart. There's nothing to be ashamed of admitting to your desires. It's totally normal and you should stop fighting…this," I said, waving my hand back and forth between us.

She shook her head at me and tossed her napkin down onto the table. "I'm not—you're mistaken about what you're thinking I want from you."

"And you're one terrible liar, Gabrielle." I lowered my voice so nobody could hear. "I have a really good memory, and I remember how you were that night in that room. With me." I nodded slowly.

"No…please don't." Her breath was coming fast and she kept shaking her head in denial, the soft ends of her mahogany hair just brushing the tops of her breasts as they rose and fell from the heavy breathing pouring from her.

I didn't let up. "How you flew apart when I made you come, the sounds you made in my mouth, my fingers tight inside you…how your tongue felt wrapped around my cock."

"Stop!" she hissed, standing up and bringing a hand to her forehead. "I have a migraine and I need to go," she blurted before leaving the table, gaining her a few looks from the others seated around us.

"Feel better, Gaby," I called after her. All for show. "Let me know if I can do *anything* to help."

She didn't turn around.

The view of her arse in that tight skirt from behind was still magnificent, and I enjoyed it thoroughly as she walked away.

I know the signs of passion in a woman's body. The flushed skin. The faltering speech. The breathing that begins in deep pulls and makes her tits heave deliciously. The guarded posture of trying to remain aloof, but knowing she's failing miserably.

My lovely obsession—the delicious Miss Gabrielle Hargreave—had every one of those signs. And I'd wager, probably an added ache up in between her thighs.

I can fix that ache for you, Gabrielle.

I'd gotten the first thing right with her tonight.

Finally.

A lethal crack in that hard shell she owned.

And for the first time in a very long while, I could say that I felt really goddamn…happy for once.

Chapter 9

Brynne had been one hundred percent correct, not that I ever doubted her. She was brilliant in her field. The larger-than-life portrait hanging in the grand stairwell at Hallborough House was a Mallerton all right. A stunning, supremely executed example from his middle period of works. Sir Jeremy Greymont and Lady Georgina Greymont with their children. God. I took it all in and enjoyed every moment of the experience.

He stood behind her as she sat in an elegantly carved chair wearing a pale pink gown and pearls.

The children, a boy and baby girl, were done as children were usually presented for the times—wide-eyed and stoic. This was early Victorian judging from the clothing. I was well aware of Mallerton's embracing of the camera obscura and figured he must have used it to paint the children and the many pets which often appeared in his works. Babies, dogs, and horses didn't stay still for long enough otherwise.

I'd have to talk to Hannah and Freddy Greymont about some archival photographs and an official cataloguing of this into the Mallerton database. I could ask Ben to take some quick prelims for me before he left. I wondered if there were any more Mallerton paintings in this house—

"You know, I have a houseful of similar portraits just waiting for you to look at them like you're studying that one right now."

I jumped at the sound of his voice right behind me.

"Oh, I know you do," I said without turning around. "I saw there were tons on the walls as I was making my escape, but I didn't have time to spare them much more than a fleeting glance."

What in the hell was he trying to do to me? Lurking around and stalking my every move, startling the bejesus out of me. I thought I'd ditched him at dinner. I really needed to stay out of his sights for the rest of the weekend as much as humanly possible. Tomorrow at the wedding was unavoidable, of course, but there would be two hundred other people around us and I'd be able to figure out some way to avoid him.

The problem with Ivan Everley was he continued to pursue me relentlessly and made that message very clear. I'm not an idiot. The man had said he wanted to fuck me when I'd been at his beloved Donadea, and it seemed nothing had changed in regards to that matter.

Had things changed for me?

You can't be with him. You can't go down that road again. Ever.

Despite his apologies and the crazy circumstances we'd both been thrown into, I just couldn't go there with him. And I wasn't sharing *why* I couldn't, either. It was better this way, and he didn't need to know my reasons. I was in charge of my body and my choices.

The hot breath of him tickled the back of my neck and I knew I was doomed when my senses reacted. That was the thing with him. He infuriated me, but my traitorous body didn't seem to be getting the memos. I couldn't help the shiver that shimmied down my spine any more than I could help how I'd been made.

I squeezed my eyes tight in an effort to ward off the arousal. To ward him off.

"It drives you crazy that you didn't get a very good look at my paintings, doesn't it, Gabrielle?"

I just stood frozen with my back to him until I felt his hands spin me around.

His eyes had a predatory gleam in them as they roved over me and he leaned in closer. I sucked in a breath.

He inhaled and gave me an eyebrow twist as if to say, "I'm waiting for an answer."

"You drive me crazier than the loss of your paintings ever will," I whispered, backing up a step, creating some needed distance between his hard body and my quivering one. I seriously couldn't handle him crowding me.

I had to get away from him before I lost my resolve—

His hand came up to under my chin and he held me to him, gentle yet firm.

"Is it bad that driving you crazy makes me feel so fucking good?" he asked before hitting me with that devastating smile which put him into mythical god territory, and me into flight mode.

I pulled myself away and ran up the stairs. And I didn't stop running until I'd reached my bedroom and could lock myself inside.

I panted behind the door, holding myself still above the pounding of my heart at the affect he had on me. I couldn't allow myself the luxury of acting upon my obvious attraction to him. Why did he continue to pursue me? Why me, in the first place? I had to keep away from him. I just had to.

It's so much safer that way.

MR. and Mrs. Blackstone were a romantic vision at their wedding. Brynne was always beautiful, and Ethan, well...he was too, but in a very male and rugged way. Right now, he looked like he'd had enough of parties and guests and anything to do with being anywhere with Brynne that wasn't private, to last him a lifetime.

I was happy for them, but I was also relieved this weekend was nearly over and I could get back to my life...and the harsh reality of a job and school. And away from Ivan Everley.

Seriously, he was dangerous.

"Simon is asking for the best man and maid-of-honor. That's you, darling," Elaina called out as she walked up with her fiancé Neil, looking happy in love with her man. They were next on the marriage circuit. Elaina had told me last night that Ivan and I would be paired up again for their wedding in six week's time. I just couldn't shake him it seemed. "Simon's making us do some crazy poses too," she added with a laugh.

"Awesome," I said to Elaina, as I made my way over to the insanely non-traditional photographer Ethan had hired—one Simon Carstairs—in his shiny custom suit of retina blinding leaf-green.

"There she is," Ivan said, holding his hand out with that deadly serious expression he liked to use on me.

What choice did I have? Be a massive bitch at my best friend's wedding, or take his hand and let him lead me around like a poodle on a leash?

His hands did a good wandering job on me, too, as Simon shouted positions for us to pose in for these ridiculous pictures. "I am not a model for Vogue," I muttered under my breath.

"But you could be. In fact, I'd even go one further and say you're far more beautiful than most of the models that grace the pages of that magazine," he whispered in my ear.

"You need to stop this...obsession...you have with me, Ivan," I hissed back.

"Good word choice. You are definitely an obsession."

"Tilt her backward Fred and Ginger style," Simon commanded.

Before I could respond Ivan had me swept beneath him, his strong arms the only thing between my ass and the garden cobblestones. He brought his forehead within an inch of mine and held me there, suspended and at his mercy.

"How's this?" He answered the photographer but he spoke the words right against my lips.

"Gorgeous, my darlings. Now bend your leg at the knee and point your toe like a dancer. You have magnificent legs, Gaby, and I need this shot. Ivan, stretch your back leg out behind you and keep it stiff."

"Oh it's definitely stiff," Ivan said softly while looking devilishly into my eyes.

Simon giggled and snapped what felt like millions of shots. "This is brilliantly luscious, you two." He kept directing us into positions that required my body to be plastered up against Ivan's tantalizing one. God, he smelled so good to me, something that hadn't changed from that first night at the National Gallery. His hair fell forward when he dipped me this way and that, brushing along his jaw and sometimes over mine. I couldn't take much more of this. It was too hard for me.

And I was starting to hate Simon-the-photographer with a passion.

"He's so right, you know."

"About?"

"Your magnificent legs." He brought his eyes down and over my bent knee and pointed toe, the effect of which had raised the wispy skirt of my dress so high he was probably seeing way more than he should.

Fuck my life.

I struggled to pull my skirt down but gravity has the ultimate say in such matters. Ivan held me how he wanted to anyway, and I sensed he wouldn't release me until he was good and ready.

"Please…Ivan, can we stop this?" I begged on a whisper. "I don't want to—I can't—please."

His gaze flickered for a moment as he held me against him, and stared down at me, weighing my request possibly?

"That's it. We've had enough," he told Simon firmly, before raising me up back to standing, his hands still holding me close, one at my lower back and the other gripping one of mine.

My dress floated back down to the floor.

"If you have a drink with me I'll stop."

"I shouldn't." I'd had several drinks tonight already but I didn't tell him that.

"But you will. I'm calling a truce with you and

it's what I want. It's time for us to make friends, Gabrielle."

"Fine." He just didn't give up and I was tired of fighting him at every turn.

When I agreed to the drink he smiled at me again, this time just as devastating to my resolve as all of the other times.

I was in very deep trouble with this man.

And he knew it as well as I did.

"YOU liked this last night so I hope another blueberry mojito is okay." I held out the glass to her as I came up to where she was waiting for me opposite the dance floor. The fact she was waiting for me at all and not trying to ditch me was a nice place to start, I thought wryly.

She accepted the drink and took a sip. "Oh, that's strong, but it's good. Thank you."

"My pleasure, of course." I tilted my head, wanting to show her I did possess some manners even if she'd never really witnessed them from me thus far. I could tell she was a complicated woman, but it was the fact she was a total mystery, that captivated me more. I needed to peel away her layers and discover her secrets one by one until there weren't any more to know. She drove me to wanting to know everything about her.

Her eyes flicked down and away from me.

My eyes on her stayed put.

I finally had her semi-alone, and since she wasn't running for the moment, I needed to get my fill of looking. The warm summer breeze fluttered her gauzy lavender dress and pressed it against the definition of her legs and breasts. Intoxicatingly female. She was also a woman very finely made.

Her hair moved, too. I wished she would look at me so I could see what was in her eyes. Eyes were sometimes all you needed to see to know how a person felt about you.

I was still trying very much to understand her motives. Why she had been so connected at the gala, and why she kept running from me now. I sensed there was far more than my error in mistaking her for an escort.

I hadn't been very successful so far but there was one thing I was dead certain about. Gabrielle Hargreave was really struggling with our attraction. It was real, and right now I could feel the heat coming off her as strong as the first time we'd met in that back gallery hallway two months ago.

"This whole thing is priceless you know, you

being Brynne's friend I was supposed to meet and ask to have a look at my paintings."

She finally let me see her eyes, but the smile she gave didn't reach them.

"Yeah, pretty much in agreement with you there," she said softly.

"Why does it make you sad, Gabrielle, because I'm not. I wanted to see you again after the gala. I tried to find you."

"I'm not sad," she said softly.

"You are. I see can see it in your eyes. But you don't have to be." I brushed a strand of hair back and tucked it behind her ear.

She froze when I touched her, a current of energy snapping between us.

She held my eyes this time. "It's mostly that I'm so ashamed of my behavior with you at the gala. That's the honest truth, Ivan. If that night had never happened then I imagine our first meeting would have gone down much differently."

She felt shame for her reaction to me in that storage closet? I didn't like that idea because shame had nothing to do with it. She'd done nothing shameful by being with me. Which left me with one conclusion as to why she was ashamed. Somebody had hurt her badly in the past and taught her to feel that way. She was far more fragile than I'd ever imagined.

I didn't like that idea, either.

"Let's walk." I held out my arm. "The lake is pretty at night with the moon and stars shining."

She eyed me and thought about it, standing there mouthwateringly gorgeous with her dress moving softly in the night breeze, holding her drink with both hands.

"It's okay; I'm completely calm and mellow right now. At your suggestion, I've been reading up on my notes from Being a Human 101."

She laughed, transferring her glass to one hand and taking my arm with the other. "I hope it helps."

"It probably won't, but I'm sure you'll tell me when I need to brush up on the main points."

"It *is* pretty out here. You were so right," she said, looking up at the full moon making the night quite bright for the lateness of the hour.

"In all things of nature there is something of the marvelous," I quoted.

"Aristotle, right?" she asked, still looking up at the sky.

"Correct." I brought my hand up to the back of her neck to steady her as we walked the footpath toward the lake.

"I had to study the classics at university much to my dismay."

"And you hated it?"

"It just didn't interest me at the time, but there was value in it I suppose. Like this lake at night with the moon and stars shining overhead."

She looked out at the view and studied it for a moment. Her beautiful face and body framed like a portrait against the night. My hand stayed put on the back of her neck, my thumb rubbing tiny circles just behind her ear.

"It *is* something of the marvelous, Ivan," she whispered up at the sky.

"I know."

She didn't even realize I was referring to her…and not the view of the lake, or the celestial night sky.

Another moment later she leaned back against my hand, and tilted her head toward me. She looked right at my lips.

I'd never look a gift-horse in the mouth, not in a situation like this one, and with Gabrielle's beautiful face turned toward mine, with an expression of desire reflected in her eyes, it was enough of a signal for me and I took it. I took her mouth.

My hand at her neck tugged and pulled her to my lips.

I heard the crash of her drink glass hitting the deck, and felt her fingers weave their way into my hair. I didn't stop. And I don't think anything could have made me stop.

I was never going to stop kissing her.

I wanted her badly, and my head was reeling at the possibilities.

Was she the woman I believed didn't exist? She was here in front of me, in my arms, my tongue in her mouth. She felt real even if my head was totally fucked up with the thoughts and ideas spinning around inside it.

She tasted like berries and rum and mint, and lush, soft female. Gabrielle Hargreave had transformed from the stiff beauty who'd just told me a few minutes ago she was ashamed of what she'd done before, into the gentle creature who now let me lead her, soft and submissive, exactly where I wanted to take her.

My bed. Her underneath me.

But there was no privacy here with so many guests everywhere poking their noses into what everyone else was doing. No, this place wouldn't work for what I wanted to do with her.

The taste of her tongue tangling with mine hit me hard in the balls and made the decision for me. The idea came all in a perfect epiphany as I heard the soft laps of Lake Leticia slapping against Nelly's floats.

I knew exactly where we were going.

Chapter 10

 "Ivan, are you sure about this?" I asked as he buckled my life vest and then did the same with the seat straps.

"Oh I'm very sure about taking you for a ride in my plane." He leaned close and kissed me expertly, leaving me breathless again. He pulled on the straps to check them and said, "Safety first, Miss Hargreave, but you're going to love this, trust me."

I still wasn't completely sure what had just happened with him. One minute he was reminding me how well he could use his lips on me, and the next he was pulling me toward his plane and asking if he could take me up for a ride.

He said, "Trust me."

Could I trust Ivan Everley? Should I trust him?

He'd looked so serious when he asked the question, holding my face in his hands and waiting for my answer. I think I would have devastated him if I'd told him no. I thought about it. I should have told him no. I think the four, or was it five, berry mojitos might have had something to do with my acquiescence, but he looked so happy when I agreed to go.

One of my many flaws is that I am a risk-taker at heart.

I'll try anything once.

So, when Ivan suggested we take a night flight in his Cessna floatplane, takeoff from the water, and look at the city lights of England under a summer full moon, I said, "why not" and let him put me in his plane. Again, the mojitos helped me come to my decision to go with him.

"You were totally right, the city lights are incredibly pretty from up here." I peered out the window thoroughly enjoying the view from the air.

"Your lack of fear impresses the hell out of me, Miss Hargreave."

"Why do you call me that all the time? It's so

formal." The alcohol had loosened my inhibitions and all kinds of questions started pouring out of me, but he didn't seem to mind answering. So, I kept asking.

"I like formalities…sometimes…as you'll learn," he said deliberately.

"Because you're a lord?"

He gave me a snort. "No, that's not why."

"Who taught you to fly a plane?"

"My uncle arranged for me to go to flight school when I was at university. He thought it was appropriate for his heir to know such things. It was something I really took to heart. I loved flying from my first lesson."

"Why did you love it?"

He shrugged. "The freedom I suppose. Troubles seem less important from up here. At least it's always felt that way to me."

"Are we flying over the ocean right now?" I couldn't see any more city lights and it made sense.

"That is the Irish Sea below us."

"Do you ever land this in the ocean?"

"No. That's the thing with floats; they only work in very calm waters. The ocean is far too rough and landing in it would not be safe, trust me."

"You keep telling me to trust you."

"I know I do." He reached his hand over to

RAINE MILLER

mine and brought it forward to rest on his lap. "Is it working?" he asked hopefully, pulling it up the rest of the way to his lips. Ahhh, so he could do romantic, too. Deadly combination Mr. Everley had going on.

"Well, I'm trying really hard to trust you. I let you take me for a ride in your plane when I could be putting my life at risk. I mean, how should I know if you're a licensed pilot and have the proper skills to land on a lake?"

He flashed me another of those teeth-baring smiles. They were very white and even, but he had the gap between the front two. Sometimes imperfections were more beautiful than the absence of them.

"You're about to find out. Here we go."

He had to release my hand to work the controls and do his checks. His hands moved in precise motions, focused and confident.

I was mesmerized as I watched him work to prepare the plane for landing.

He banked toward the left before leveling it out to descend rapidly and drop us just a few feet over the dark water of the lake. We skimmed along for a bit until the swoosh of water grabbed the bottom of the floats and immediately slowed our momentum. In a matter of seconds we were no longer propelled through the air, but floating in water and gliding along smoothly like a sailboat.

Amazing.

"Wow, that was so—so awesome." And I really meant it.

"So, you enjoyed that, did you?"

"Yes. It was beautiful."

He looked at me and said, "You're beautiful."

That he thought so made me feel good inside, but still I had to look away. Whatever we were doing was still too new for me to process completely and made me feel shy. Plus all of those drinks…

I focused on what was outside my window instead. The landscape looked different to me from when we'd taken off from Hallborough. The lake looked bigger and there were far fewer lights than I remembered. Only the moon lit up the night sky.

"Did you land us on the other side of the lake from where we took off, or something?" I asked.

"You could say that."

"Oh…"

I was confused but he seemed to know what he was doing as he steered the plane along through the water. After a few minutes he slowed and carefully navigated toward what looked like a concrete ramp. The sound of wheels turning as tires met a hard surface surprised me. He drove the plane right out of the water and onto a dry dock that seemed to be specially built for the purpose. It had a roof and everything. Like a parking spot for a plane.

This wasn't Hallborough at all.

"We're not at Hallborough anymore." My words sounded as if I was trying to convince myself.

Trying to convince myself that I hadn't just been kidnapped.

"No, not Hallborough," he said clearly.

"Where have you brought me, Ivan?" I could hear the panic in my own voice.

"Remember what I told you at dinner last night? That you would come back after the wedding? Well, the wedding is over."

"Ivan, where have you brought me?" I repeated the question even though I had a pretty good idea. And my voice had moved past panic and off into HystericalLand.

"Donadea," he whispered.

"You fucking bastard!"

He grabbed me by the shoulders and forced me to look at him.

"I want you to listen to me before you have another freak out, okay?"

"You have to take me back to Hallborough, Ivan."

"I will. I promise you I will take you back, but

just not tonight. Gabrielle, please—please give me this night. With you…here."

I tried to understand what he was asking.

"You said you were ashamed of what we did before and I gather you have your reasons. I'm not ashamed of anything we did together that night. I want to do more. Much more, Gabrielle."

I struggled to get out of his grip on me but my senses were dulled from the alcohol.

"Just listen for a moment."

"No, you tricked me—"

He slammed his lips against mine to shut me up. It worked. And once he started in with the nibbling and sucking on my bottom lip I no longer wanted to get away. His kisses drugged me into compliance and took me to a place where I didn't have to think about anything, or make difficult decisions. I could just feel good.

But Ivan knew all of this about me already.

"Here we can be totally private and nobody will ever have to know. If that's what you want, we can do this in secret and not tell anyone. This is Northern Ireland—a virtual wilderness."

"Ivan…"

"Just me and you doing what we've wanted to do from that first night. I'm right, aren't I?"

I took a deep breath and drew up a finger to

move his hair behind his ear. It felt so good to touch him, and he *was* right.

"Give me the rest of the weekend alone with you," he told me as he pulled the palm of my hand to his cheek and held it there.

"I don't have any clothes."

He smirked and tilted his head. "You won't need them."

"You just want to fuck me, Ivan." I waited for his response to my statement, watching his eyes for the truth.

He shook his head sharply. "No, that's not completely true. I want to get to know you and…explore…what I think we have going on already." He held one side of my face with his other hand and said the rest. "In addition to the fucking. I want to do that, too. Over and over again, I'll admit."

His eyes seared me while my brain conjured all sorts of pornographic images of him and me doing that very thing. What would it be like with him?

And I truly did want to know how it would be.

I shivered at his blunt speech. At least he was being honest with me about his desires. Did I dare give him back the same honesty?

"If there's anything you don't want to do just tell me. I'll respect it. I follow the rules," he said carefully, his hand still holding my face, his thumb rubbing my jaw.

Rules. I'd pledged to rules before and it involved not going into another entanglement like Ivan was offering.. And this was what he was suggesting to me. I understood him crystal clear. He was a dominant in the bedroom, and he was very aware of what I was, too. Could I do sex just for the pleasure of it with no emotional attachments? I didn't even know if I could.

"Trust me, Gabrielle. That's all you have to do right now. We have to begin somewhere and I'm asking you to start by trusting me for just this one night."

"I'm afraid of trusting a man again," I whispered.

"I can tell, and it bothers me. Very much," he said softly as he pulled me under his lips with a hand at the back of my neck. His kiss was sweet at first, but then he opened his mouth wide and covered mine completely, plunging his tongue inside in an act of dominance that stole away my hesitation in the same moment as he took control.

When he was finished with the kiss he held my face firmly with both of his hands. "I know you want this. I know you're curious. I know I can't stop thinking about you. I don't want to stop," he said harshly, "I want to go all the way with you until we both know what that feels like." He whispered, "I know it will feel so good."

His deep green eyes searched mine, his thumbs brushed along my cheekbones, his body throbbed along with my heart—and I knew I was going to agree.

"So, can we do this, my lovely Miss Hargreave?"

I closed my eyes in a pathetic attempt to find some strength but there was none to be had. I wanted to be with him, too. Was he really handing this decision over to me though? He was such an attraction to me and had been from the first moment I ever laid eyes on him. I wanted to know what it felt like to have him over me at least once. I wanted to find that place in my head my body craved, and I tried to deny. I wanted to go there with this beautiful man who kept telling me I was beautiful to him. I wanted to be with Ivan Everley more than I'd ever wanted to be with any man. And nobody would have to know. We were all alone here at Donadea, and that did take away a lot of my hesitation.

"Don't shut your eyes," he said, his head dipping down ready to make eye contact the second I followed his command and opened them. "I need to see those green beauties on me when you say yes."

I sucked in a sharp breath and got lost in his dark green ones.

Priceless

"You can have carte blanche with my paintings if you like. No pressure, but maybe you'll find something that interests you and you'll want to stay longer."

God, he really had the art of persuasion down to a tee. He could pull out all the stops when he wanted. He also knew what made me tick, and lucky for him, had the goods in his pocket to offer up. It had been such a long time since I'd felt beautiful in the eyes of a man, and Ivan kept telling me so often it was hard to push him away. Even if only for one night, he would make me feel alive and beautiful. One night was all I deserved. I'd have to be content with that.

"No, just for tonight," I told him. "Tomorrow you take me back to Hallborough and nobody knows we ever did this."

"Is that a yes?"

I nodded. "But, Ivan, you need to know...I'm scared," I blurted honestly. It was the truth and he should know it coming from me.

"Of me?" He frowned, looking bothered by my declaration.

"No." I shook my head. "I'm scared of me."

Chapter 11

She felt scared. Afraid of letting her inhibitions run free. I could understand that bit. I'd felt the same way before. Many times. But the prospect of being with Gabrielle didn't scare me. That wasn't my issue at all. I was very determined not to fuck up with her again.

Fuck? Definitely yes.

Fuck up? Not happening this time.

Go slow. Tell her what you want. Find out what she needs. Give it to her.

"Shhh, don't be scared." I brought her to my lips and kissed her gently, thrilling at the soft trace of her tongue responding to my lead. She was going to be perfect. "Not of yourself, and not of me, okay?" I asked, dipping down to find her eyes.

"All right," she breathed. I could feel her trembling underneath my hands. What she didn't know was her trembling was just the beginning of what I was going to pull out of her tonight.

"What do you say to getting out of this flying boat and up to the house?"

She nodded "yes" but didn't say anything as I unbuckled her from the seat and stowed her life jacket. She watched my hands, and for some reason it was so fucking sexy coming from her.

I would be doing a lot of things to her with my hands in a little while, and once I got started I wasn't going to stop until I was good and ready to stop, and she was exhausted from the many orgasms I'd give her.

And she would take all of it from me.

I could hardly believe she was really here at all, and I couldn't resist another kiss before leaving the plane from my pilot's seat. She tasted sweet. So soft. It was hard to reconcile her with the feisty creature I'd met on the road the time she'd come here before. And she was so different with me right now. A side of her I'd not seen before, and made me want her so badly, I could've gone for a quick grind right here in the back of the plane just to take the edge off.

"I'll come around to your side and help you out, okay?"

"All right," she said, bringing a finger to her lips, touching where my tongue had just been.

My dick was brutally stiff to the point it hurt to move, but move I did. I needed her up in my bed like two months ago.

I opened the door for her. "Just step onto the base of the doorway." I held my arms up.

One long leg came into view and then the other as she stood up and balanced on the edge, her heels framing her feet while the dress fluttered against that banging hot body I couldn't wait to see naked.

She was a fucking vision. Portrait worthy.

"I've got you," I said, as I took her behind the knees with one arm while the other wrapped around her back, and just like that she was in my arms smelling sexy and sweet like berries.

Her hand gripped the back of my shoulder, the pressure of her holding onto me feeling fucking perfect. I didn't want to set her down straight away. She felt so right in my arms.

"How do we get to the house?" She rolled one of her ankles and showed off what, if I had to guess, were steely grey Manolo Blahnik with an open toe, and very sexy on her feet. "I don't think these will make it very far, and I really like them."

I laughed. "I really like them, too."

"Are you going to carry me?" she asked coyly.

"I'd rather not."

"Chivalry has died so soon, Mr. Everley. So sad." She mocked a sad shake of her head that made my cock even more twitchy.

"No, Miss Hargreave, it has not died actually, but I am afraid my arms will die if I have to carry you the two miles distance it will take to get us to my house."

She frowned adorably. "But I can't ruin my shoes."

I kissed her, licking along her bottom lip until she opened for my tongue. It was hard not to put her back in the plane and stretch her out in the rear cargo where I could get acquainted with her body sans the pretty dress. She could even keep her shoes on if she liked.

But that wasn't how this night was going to go down. No, I had special plans for my Gabrielle.

My?

Fuckin' hell, I surely hoped so. It had taken close to a miracle for me to find her again.

With some superhuman effort, I pulled away from her luscious lips and carried her to the Jeep parked on the other side of the hangar. I set her down carefully and motioned with my arm. "My lady, your chariot awaits and your precious shoes will be spared."

"Ah, but what you really mean is your precious arms will be spared." She teased me with a soft draw of her finger down the sleeve of my jacket.

"Of course." I gave her a wink. "I don't want to waste all my energy up carrying you two miles over hill and dale when I could be using that same effort for *other* things."

The sexual tension exploded between us as soon as the words left my mouth.

One second we were teasing each other, and the next second we definitely weren't.

She reached for the door handle at the same moment I did, our hands colliding.

Fuck this, I thought. Fumbling around was time wasted when I could be getting lost in her.

I put her in the Jeep, and had myself behind the wheel with the ignition on about five seconds after that.

Yeah, she was going to be mine all right. At least for tonight she would. Gabrielle was on the exact same page as me with the sex.

As I floored the Jeep up the dirt road to the house, I had to ask myself one really important question.

Was I ready to do this again? Because once I started down this path with her I wouldn't be able to shut it off and stop. I knew she wasn't at all like the women who'd distracted me since Viviana. Deep down in my bones I knew it. Gabrielle would ignite in me emotions I'd buried because I understood precisely what they did to me. She'd begin a change in me. I'd get possessive, and needy, and controlling. My kink would emerge. Those things I couldn't alter about myself. Is that what drew me to her so strongly? Were we both feeling an innate sense of connection here? But what if I was way off base? She might not want me once she met *that* Ivan Everley.

But it would be too late by that point.

She didn't know it, but Gabrielle wasn't the only one who'd been burned for trusting someone.

I looked over at her sitting beautifully calm beside me. Gabrielle had already made her decision to be with me. Her struggle had come before, and emotionally was behind her now.

That's when I knew the reality of my situation.

It was too late for me already. She'd already unknowingly begun the change. Whether she wanted it or not, I was already hers.

I led her up the stairs quickly, her left hand clasped firmly in my right, and her Manolos clutched in my other. I was impatient and didn't want her stumbling or twisting her ankle going up the massive staircase in those high heels. I'd put them back on her later. When she was gloriously naked.

This reminded me of the other time I'd led her by the hand. When I brought her in from the garage through the pouring rain. I wondered if she remembered. But that time was very different from right now. This time I was taking her to my bedroom where we would fuck wildly and have a mutually pleasurable time together. *Finally*. Two people on a mission to fornicate in the dirtiest ways possible, I hoped.

I brought her to my door and then drew her inside with me. I dropped her shoes and turned the lock, the mechanism sliding into its place a symbolic gesture. There was no turning back now. We were doing this.

"Step into the middle," I told her. "I want to be able to see every inch of you in the light."

So we begin.

She went forward slowly as I'd asked, standing calmly, and waiting for my lead.

Fucking perfection.

I was behind her in two steps. Close. Inhaling her scent, my lips hovering over her neck.

My fingers found the zip of her dress and took it down.

My palms moved under the fabric to her bare shoulders so I could push the sleeves over and off.

My hands swept down the length of her arms all the way to find her fingers so I could intertwine them with mine.

Her dress slid down to the floor to land in a puddle around our feet.

I lifted her arms above her head and spun her around to face me.

My eyes swept over her and took in her exquisite feminine beauty. Long legs attached to a slim waist with hips generous enough for my hands to grip when my cock was driving into her. And gorgeous tits. I still hadn't seen them yet. Right now they were encased in a lavender lace bra but I knew they were magnificent. I had to fight to keep myself from ripping those bits of lace off her. *Patience, you have her all night.*

I released her hands from over her head and brought her arms down to rest at her sides. I stepped back just a bit, even though it was hard to move away from her. I needed a better view for what was coming next.

"Take off the rest." My words had an edge now. I couldn't help it. The instant we'd stepped in here together and locked the door behind us, everything changed.

I understood. She understood. We found our roles and slipped into our places. The ambiance of *we're-about-to-fuck* swirled around us in the room.

Gabrielle reached around her back with delicate hands and found the hooks of her bra. She released them in succession—one, two, three—small clicks I heard clearly in the otherwise silence of my bedroom. She raised and then rolled her shoulders forward until the straps slid down her arms. She held that position for a moment, as I held my breath, for one last second of modesty before letting the lavender lace drop away to land atop her dress already on the floor.

I stood there gaping at perfection. I knew I'd never have my fill of looking at her breasts. The most beautiful pair I think I'd ever seen in my life. Honest to God, straight-up truth. They were full but not heavy, completely round with lush soft tips, and certified, one-hundred-percent natural. I knew real from fake. I knew something else, too. I was in love with her tits. Total and complete love affair going on between that twin pair of beauties and me.

I gorged myself on looking, hoping I didn't have drool coming off my chin. Her dark pink nipples went from soft to hardening into tight buds right before my eyes. And her nipples weren't the only thing that was hard. I had a raging hard-on straining painfully against the fly of my trousers. I wanted to see her eyes on my cock and know she was the one who made it hard. To know what *she* did to me.

I still had on my tuxedo from the wedding. All she wore was lavender lace knickers—a thong at that. Christ, I might just go blind tonight.

"Everything. Off."

She deftly placed her thumbs underneath the lace and drew downward, the delicate fabric rolling into a twisted band that skimmed over her lean thighs…before sliding down the rest of the distance to meet the floor and the rest of her clothes.

She stepped out of the pile of fabric at her feet, completely naked in front of me.

Clothed only in the soft waves of her mahogany hair.

It took me a moment to find my voice. It took another moment to control myself from pulling her beneath me and finding that warm, pulsing place to put my cock.

I clenched my hands and came up with four words that summed everything up about Gabrielle

Hargreave and what she was to me.

"Something of the marvelous."

I held out my hand, beckoning her. She took slow sultry steps toward me. The effect of her completely naked while I was still fully clothed wound me up so tight I thought my spine might snap from the tension.

Fuck me…

She. Was. Beautiful.

No—beautiful was a pitiful word to describe what she was.

Exquisite—Flawless—Resplendent—were better. But just barely.

"I don't even have words for you right now."

She smiled as she took her last step and put her hand in mine. I pulled her into my body and took her mouth, going deep this time, my tongue desperate to be in her. I slid my hands down to cup the curves of her arse and lifted her. She wrapped her legs around my hips and gripped me tightly. My straining cock pressed in right between her legs, our bodies interlocking perfectly. She thrust against the ridge of my erection as I held her up. I groaned right into her mouth. She did the same, her hands buried deep into my hair, as she seemed inclined to do whenever I kissed her. We ground against each other, battling tongues in a desperate attempt to merge our bodies. I wanted inside her as much as she wanted me in her. The knowledge fueled me. This was no timid inexperienced girl in my arms. She was a woman well aware of what she wanted. Thank the fuckin' gods.

Somehow—I have no idea how—I walked us to the bed, managed to set her on the edge of it, and backed up a few steps. My cock pounded to get to her, but there was other territory to claim on her first before my cock got into the action.

"Arms up over your head. Feet apart. Knees together. And don't take your eyes off me."

She did all of that for me, arranging herself elegantly—waiting—her seductive eyes watching my every move. She appeared to hold no insecurity in her nakedness at all, which was a nuclear hot turn-on for me. Here, in this room, she was a sensual goddess completely at ease in her skin, allowing me to take control of the pleasure for the both of us. This. *This* is the woman I met at the gallery.

"You're so fucking perfect, Gabrielle. So goddamn sexy right now. I want to give *you* something. What can I do for *you*?"

She told me without a trace of hesitation. "I

want you naked. I want to see you. You can strip down for me."

Fuck yeeeees. A woman who knows what she wants and knows how to ask for it.

I gave it to her. I did it a helluva lot faster than she had done it, my execution ridiculously sloppy. The Brunello Cucinelli jacket I'd worn for the wedding probably screeched in horrified protest as I wrenched it off my back with the sleeves inside out before flinging it carelessly to the floor. Jackets costing fifteen hundred quid didn't concern me in the slightest right now. Cost was immaterial when I was giving her something she wanted, something she'd asked of me.

Her eyes flared wide and her eyebrows went up when I dropped my shorts and she got the full-frontal Ivan in ready position. Did excellent things for my ego, too. I knew I had a big cock, but what was more important than the size was that I knew well how to use it. She had nothing to worry about.

When she licked her lips deliberately, looking wistfully at my tackle for a moment before tearing her eyes away to give me a sultry little grin, I knew she wasn't intimidated by the size of my cock at all. I might be the one who needed to worry.

Fuck me into next Friday, where had she been all my life? I'd found the woman of my every wet-dream fantasy come true right here.

"You're beautiful, Ivan. A beautiful man," she said clearly. Her eyes held onto mine as I'd told her to earlier, but I was the one finding it difficult to keep to my own rule. Her praise got to me, made it difficult not to look away, but that would've been a travesty if I'd done it because she wasn't finished with her tantalizing sex show.

I watched as Gabrielle boldly slid her spectacular arse backward up my bed, stretched out her magnificent long legs, and propped herself into a reclining position resting on her elbows.

A mischievous come-hither look in my direction. The slow circling of an ankle. The sexy roll of a shoulder. A soft laugh.

I knew what she was going to do and I held my breath waiting for it.

One knee bent. And then the other. Right foot planted to the side. And then the left.

She gave it all up for my private viewing pleasure.

And it was indeed my pleasure.

Her pussy…became my total delicious pleasure. Bare and smooth. Dark pink petals wet with arousal waiting for me to give them a kiss.

If my heart didn't give out and kill me before I could claim it.

I had my face between her thighs licking at the folds of her pussy until they opened up under my tongue and I could get to her clit - that tiny pleasure centre to which I'd be devoting some special attentions to tonight. Fortunately for me.

I couldn't get enough of the taste of her cunt. The taste, the sight, or the feel of what I had up against my mouth.

She rocked her hips into a rhythm in perfect step with what I was doing, building her closer to her peak with every flick of my tongue. I needed to feel her coming under my mouth first. We could fuck afterward. We were going to be at this for a while and there was no rush. I don't know why I needed it in that order, but I did.

I held her open with my hands on her inner thighs and pinned to my bed, totally at my mercy while I gave her my best. Gabrielle made quiet sounds, soft, breathy moans that traveled directly into my ears on the eroticism contained within them. I heard every whimper and soft shuddering sigh as if she'd screamed them in her pleasure. It took me a few minutes but I got those screams out of her, too. I worked my tongue a little harder, a little deeper, a little more of everything, until I was rewarded with the sound of her begging me not to stop and she was indeed crying my name.

"Don't worry, baby, I'm not stopping. You're going again."

She shuddered a drawn out keening cry when the second orgasm followed right on top of the first. "Oh, Gooooooooooood, Ivaaaaaaaan!"

I pressed the flat of my tongue over her clit and held it firm and tight as she rode out round two. She writhed through the crest and then the crash, pulling on my hair with clenched hands. Even though I'd directed her to have her hands above her head, it just didn't matter. Sex with Gabrielle was something completely unprecedented, new territory for me, and sexy as all fuck.

After she let go of my hair, I gave her pussy one last gentle suck before moving up the bed beside her.

I gathered her up and against me where I could really see her.

She panted in deep breaths, her eye makeup all mussed and streaked from the tears that had leaked out of her eyes during the orgasms. Her nipples were hardened, and rose and fell with her breasts as she breathed. Just stunning.

My God. There just weren't words for how beautiful she looked, or how I felt seeing her like this in my arms.

I gripped her chin harshly with one hand and took her mouth again. One penetration exchanged for another. As much of her as I could get. She melted underneath me, taking it all so perfectly, everything I did to her, everything I demanded from her.

When I was able, I dragged my mouth away and looked down.

I still hadn't had any time with my favorites yet. I guess I'd been savoring the anticipation of getting acquainted with her glorious tits, but it was well past time for us to be introduced.

I palmed one side, learning the weight, and the incredible softness. Beauteous perfection filled one hand, while the sweetest taste of a budded nipple burst in my mouth. I sucked and nipped, pulled and kissed and pinched. I even used my teeth on them. I couldn't help half of the moves I made over her. I feasted and indulged in her body and got lost in the sweet and beautiful compliance she gave up to me.

When I felt her hands buried in my hair again I just couldn't wait any longer.

"Are you ready for me because I want to fuck you now, Gabrielle."

"Yes, please." She shifted her legs beneath me to make room.

"It won't be gentle because I know I can't do it that way right now. I'm dyin' for you."

"But I don't want you gentle," she said clearly, her eyes hooded in desire, her neck arched to one side. "I want to feel you over me—inside me. I want that, Ivan."

I kissed her quickly before hopping off the bed to find my trousers. Condoms. I needed one and was pretty sure the only place there were any to be had was in my wallet. I never brought women to Donadea, thus was not prepared for this sex-a-thon currently in play.

I spotted the other half of my Brunello Cucinelli in disarray, trouser legs split apart and draped over my green chair inside out. I snatched them up and headed back toward the bed where Gabrielle was waiting for me to fuck her senseless.

She most certainly was. Gabrielle studied me, her eyes tracking my movements, assessing what I was on about, figuring out what I was searching for. I winked at her as I dug around in the pocket until I found my wallet. She smiled in that quiet way of hers, waiting patiently.

Two.

Only two foil packets in there. Two condoms were not going to be enough, I realized. Not with her. We'd have to get creative or get some more from someplace.

I waved the packets in the air so she could see I'd had good success, but she was no longer lying back and waiting patiently. She was now sitting up in the bed with her hand out toward me. "I want to put it on you. Please?"

Her request thrilled me because it told me she wanted her hands on my cock. I wanted her hands on my cock. Her *anything* on my cock would do nicely right now.

"As you wish, lovely thing." I handed her one packet and watched her small hands open the foil and remove the condom.

She reached forward tentatively with the other and took a firm hold of my rock-hard shaft. I hissed, unable to control the thrust that pushed me sliding against her palm. The smile on her face just about did me in. That, and the slow lick she gave the bell end before rolling the wrap down my aching length.

Patience fell away then. I was desperate to bury myself in her. I pressed her back into the bed and stretched her arms up over her head.

She said nothing but I saw the fire in her eyes. This first fuck was going to be very, very nice. For both of us.

I gathered her knees up from underneath and spread her wide, ready and waiting for me to sink into her.

The tip of my cock was guided to her center and pressed in softly at first. Wet pussy gave in to the pressure and took me all the way to the root on one hard thrust. I hadn't lied. This first time couldn't be gentle. It would be hard and pounding, almost a punishment for having to wait so long for it.

We both shouted I think. I held the top of her head and checked her face to see if she was with me. She thrust up on my cock and looked at me with eyes already lost to the heat of sexual pleasure, and gave me her answer. She wanted everything I would give her.

"Fuuuuuuck, that's good," I said as I started to move. Deep, full, plunges into her over and over until everything else disappeared from thought and nothing else existed except her cunt and my cock fitting together in the most primal way possible. Hard moving into soft. A key inserted into a lock. An arrow shot into a target.

An arrow into a heart...

In metaphor, I would be the arrow while the heart would represent female, but as I melded into her, and felt the burn of an impending cataclysm that would only leave me hungry for more of her, I knew the metaphor of a heart and an arrow didn't apply in the usual way.

Gabrielle was my arrow, and the…heart? The heart was me. The heart was *me*.

Chapter 12

Ivan in the grips of an orgasm was something pretty beautiful. I couldn't take my eyes away from the sight of him. Of us, of our bodies fitting together like they were predestined for it. When his long fingers reached down and rubbed over my clit I knew I was coming with him.

I'd lost count of how many times he had made me come. By orgasm count, our numbers were seriously uneven, though.

The familiar tightening and flicker of desperation

hit me hard. Just as hard as he was pounding his cock into me.

"Ooooooooh!" I moaned on a drawn-out wail as the pleasure broke over me, in me, through me, and I was carried along in a current of something much bigger than myself.

"Yeah—yeah you are!" he said harshly, green eyes drilling into mine as I felt his cock swell and tighten even more inside me. His hair whipped back and forth as he pistoned his hips, driving us both. "Fuck!" he shouted on one last near-painful thrust, burying his cock to the hilt as his orgasm detonated, the green fire in his eyes holding me captive so I was incapable of looking away.

We both panted and stared at each other allowing the pleasure to roll over us both.

At some point, I felt him move off me and roll to the side of the bed. He stripped off the condom and did something with it before turning back to me and gathering me close against his chest.

I should probably get up and dressed I thought, but I didn't want to. My eyes were already closing, and I was feeling blissfully content for the first time in longer than I could remember. I don't think I'd ever felt quite like this after sex with anybody. Strong, muscled arms held onto me, a male-scented chest of clean sweat and lingering sex warmed my cheek, long fingers caressed my back and shoulder, and soft lips, framed in beard stubble, pressed against my forehead.

Ivan had been so right.

Doing this with him had felt so good.

I left the bed carefully so I wouldn't wake her up. I was on a mission of great importance. Really fucking vital you might say.

I found my reading glasses and my mobile and texted Lowell. **Have condoms delivered to Donadea residence ASAP. This is an URGENT matter. -I Everley**

My assistant was quirky but he did everything I asked without question. I had no qualms making requests to him for anything. I could count the non-family members I trusted implicitly on one hand, and Lowell Brinkley was on that list.

My mobile buzzed. **What kind would you like? -Lowell Brinkley, Administrative Assistant to Mr. Ivan Everley, Lord Rothvale XIII**

I rolled my eyes at the ridiculously absurd signature he attached to his messages and realized the part about him never questioning me wasn't quite true. **The kind that will cover my cock.   -I Everley**

I silenced my mobile and studied Gabrielle sleeping in my bed. It was all I wanted to do right now - look at her. She had mesmerized me from our first meeting up until this very second. What we had done here together last night was something I'd never forget. Being with her was also an experience unlike anything I'd ever had with a woman. There had been many women, and I'd enjoyed a lot of sex over the years, before and after my disastrous marriage. I could say for certain that not one of those women was anything like Gabrielle.

I drew my fingertip over her cheekbone and moved a bit of hair that had fallen over her face back behind her ear. She stirred a little but didn't wake up or open her eyes.

I settled back into the bed beside her and got comfortable. I thought about the idea of what being with her last night had meant to me.

Somehow, it felt wonderful and terrifying both at the same time.

I found myself in a very modern bedroom

completely out of character from the rest of the Georgian mansion I'd visited before. The bed coverings were sumptuous, classic white duvet and pillows, but it was the chair in the corner that really caught my eye. Leather, tufted, massive in size, and an unusual color. An intense green that almost didn't fit. Almost. Because that chair *did* fit him actually.

Lord Ivan had a lordly chair in his bedroom.

"She awakens."

I smiled and turned to find him on his side looking at me with an elbow propping him up.

"Looking" wasn't really the proper word, though. To describe what he was doing right now, devouring would be more accurate. Ivan devoured my body with his eyes, and the effect was totally empowering to me for some reason. It didn't make me feel self-conscious because I knew he liked what he saw.

It was weird to wake up naked in bed with him after a night of mind-blowing sex and not have it feel awkward. But it wasn't at all. Must have been the secret nature of our whole agreement. The *nobody has to know* and the *we can do what we've wanted to do together from the beginning and keep it totally private* parts of the equation that made everything feel so comfortable with him.

"How long have you been staring at me

sleeping?"

He spoke softly. "I've no idea; I just know I've been very much enjoying the view." His eyes moved down to caress my breasts and then a lazy stroll back on up to my face eventually. Not one ounce of contrition on his handsome face either.

I raised an eyebrow. "Is that so?"

He cracked a one-sided grin. "Oh yes," he said quietly, keeping still and just content to watch me. I got the idea Ivan was a bit of a voyeur. He was a watcher. And he got off on it. Some of the things I'd done last night, and his reaction to me, told me this was a primal truth about him.

I felt a blush heat my face and peeked a glance at him. Remembering the things I'd done. The things Ivan had done to me. Last night had put me in the crazy-wild corner for a few hours, but it had been so good. I doubt any of it would have happened without the influence of some really killer berry mojitos, either.

"What's on your mind, Miss Hargreave?" he asked with a twinkle in his eye.

Of course he knew I was remembering last night. Probably was reading my mind right now, too. "Oh, nothing of any importance," I said with a slight shake of my head.

"Really. So why the pretty blush then?" He

trailed one finger down from my cheek to circle between my breasts and gave me a flash of a smirk.

I decided to have a little fun with him.

"It probably has something to do with a dream I had."

"Do you remember this dream?" he asked.

"Most of it." I nodded.

"Tell me."

"It was so weird. I was at my best friend's wedding minding my own business, and enjoying some blueberry mojitos." I blinked a few times at him. "I might have overindulged a bit on the alcohol. Probably had at least four of the mojitos…and this is where it gets really fuzzy in my memory." I rubbed my head in confusion as if I was having trouble remembering. "But I could swear that the best man at the wedding, Lord Everinghamwich of Donagolia, or something like that." I waved my hand in dismissal. "Not important, a minor detail…but anyway, this Lord Everinghamwich stalked me the whole time at the reception. I mean I could *not* shake the guy off me for anything. He asked me to dance three times, and when I finally agreed to one quick spin around the dance floor, he spent the entire time trying to have a look up my dress." I giggled and gave him a little shove in the shoulder. "The naughty man thought he would try to kidnap me and take me away to his castle in Donagolia." I gave a shocked face. "In a blimp." I shook my head enthusiastically. "I'm not kidding, I remember it was a blimp because he stole my Manolo Blahniks off my feet and threw them in the lake. He said the heels would pop a hole in his blimp if I wore them in there." I tried to keep a straight face and finish my tale before I lost the ability. I couldn't even risk a glimpse at his face because I knew I'd lose it. "So, while we were up in the air he led me to believe he was kidnapping me so he could...you know...try for some more sexy time with me because he was under the assumption I might be a prostitute." I snorted in laughter. "I didn't realize it at the time, but I had no cause to worry about Lord Ev *at all* because he only wanted to bring me to his castle so he could show me his rare collection of miniature balls. He gave me a special *tour*." I made dramatic air quotes with my fingers and winked. "Took hours to see it all. They just looked like regular old marbles to me but he kept insisting they were tiny balls—"

Ivan was laughing loudly when he pounced on me and ended my little storytelling adventure. His big body swallowed me up as he got in some evil tickling. I shrieked and tried to wriggle away but he was far too fast for me. "Tiny balls, huh?"

I nodded, laughing up at him. "Yes. But he had a lot of them. Quantity more than made up for what they lacked in size. But man, yeah they were really tiny."

"You are a devil woman," he said shaking his head in amusement. "And that was quite a creative tale you've just wove together on the fly. I am impressed again, Miss Hargreave."

"Thank you, Mr. Everley. And you totally deserved it for leering at me while I was sleeping and naked."

"Now, I cannot help that. Come on, you're naked in my bed and I'm supposed to avert my eyes or something?" he complained.

"That would be the gentlemanly thing to do, yes."

"Well good then, because we've already established I am no gentleman." His eyes darkened. "So I'll continue my leering whenever you are naked in my bed, thank you very much." He took my face and pulled me up to his, eyes dead serious. "I won't look away from you, Gabrielle, unless I'm dead."

In a matter of seconds we went from horsing around and giggling, to passionate kissing as a prelude to more sex, when he dropped his lips to mine and covered my whole mouth forcefully with his. He kissed me harshly, demandingly erotic as he pressed down into me with an erection that hit me right where it felt so good. Ivan made everything he did feel so good.

The sheets were ripped aside and he made his way to my breasts. He sucked on one and held the other, pinching and twisting the nipple over and over until I was gasping from the sweet pleasure-pain it produced and shaking underneath him.

He pulled up to his knees abruptly, and reached for the other packet on the bedside table. This time he sheathed himself while I watched the show. And the show was quite impressive because Ivan had a huge cock. Biggest one I'd ever met. I'd noticed the size of him last night when he'd stripped down for me. No micro-penis for this British hottie. He could rate with the record holders. But despite his size, he was well proportioned, long and thick with a slight curve to the left, and trimmed up neatly. For a penis it was quite beautiful, and lord knows he could do amazing things with it. I'd learned this lesson last night.

I waited as he stared darkly into my eyes. When it came down to the actual sex, Ivan became serious, almost menacing in his demeanor. It was the hottest thing I'd ever experienced with a man. The anticipation of waiting for him to start in on me made me ache, wondering what he would do, or demand from me.

Without warning he flipped me over. On my knees, he pushed down on my shoulders so my ass was up in the air. I knew he was staring again, seeing the unique parts of a woman's body that make a man want to fuck her like the caveman he is at heart.

I felt fingers stroking and penetrating, making me ready for him. He found my clit and rubbed the tip of his cock over it back and forth until I was on the edge of desperation and literally shaking under him.

"You're so fucking gorgeous like this." He spoke reverently but harshly, his words piercing into my consciousness right along with his huge, beautiful cock.

He filled me up so completely, I couldn't help crying out loudly. He held himself in me and slid his hands to the sides of my hips, his fingers biting into my flesh, owning my body, sending the message I was at his mercy until he deemed it at an end. Until he'd forced another climax or two out of me and was ready to give into his own.

I could only hold on as he pumped his cock in and out of me, so deep and so hard from this angle, it felt like I would break apart at any second. Only his firm grip on my hips held me down. I flew so high from the pleasure of him in me I think I would have floated away if he wasn't holding onto me so tightly.

The sounds of our bodies hitting together, his tortured groans, my heavy gasps, notched up the heat of the sex even more. Just seconds after he'd made me come, and he was on the verge of his own orgasm, Ivan said something that cut right to the heart of the matter with us. He pulled on my hair and drew my neck back, speaking the words into my ear as he continued on with the fierce fucking. He said, "I own this body of yours when I have my cock in you." And he was right.

He did own my body in that moment, even if I would have given it to him freely.

He absolutely did.

His cock swelled impossibly harder as he thrust into me with an almost agonized sounding groan, holding me impaled as he finally came. His teeth bit into my shoulder just enough to bring a sharp sting of delicious pain before he soothed over the spot with his tongue.

When he released me, the ominous Ivan disappeared and the gentle Ivan reemerged. He held me the same way he had last night, caressing and combing fingers through my hair. Being in his arms afterward was again, something I'd not really experienced before. It was new to me, but I loved it.

He made me feel so precious, like I was important to him—special. It scared me only because I responded so powerfully to his attentions. Almost like an instant addiction for people who sample a drug for the first time. It was like that for me with Ivan.

This was only supposed to be one night of letting my inhibitions fly and not have the guilt to contend with by being done in private. But fate had played a dirty trick on me I now realized. And too much alcohol had helped me to make stupid decisions that I couldn't take back now, or ever.

I had been with Ivan. I now knew what that felt like.

Like something very wonderful.

And I knew I'd wish for more time with him once he took me back to Hallborough later today and said goodbye.

Even so, I stayed exactly where I was, cuddled up against his muscled chest with his arm around me. I breathed in the scent of him so I could hold onto the good feelings for just a little longer. Maybe I deserved more than just one night with him...

What are you doing, Gabrielle?

Chapter 13

After the good-morning-fuck, we dozed a bit. We needed it. The sex was intense with her, and a little rest helped us both come down to earth afterward.

It was already beginning.

The change in me I was worried about.

But I knew I couldn't do a thing about it anymore than I could get enough of Gabrielle Hargreave. I wished I could make time slow because the sands in the hourglass were pouring out far too quickly for me. I dreaded the moment when she would say I had to take her back to London where she lived and worked.

I didn't want to take her back.

I didn't even want to go back to London because I knew everything would be different there. It wouldn't be like this was here with her right now. Easy. So good. Fun.

I wanted her to stay at Donadea with me so I could hear her tell more outrageously mocking fairy tales. To hear the sound of her teasing in that California-girl American accent she spoke in. To laugh together in bed over funny, stupid, nothingness. To watch her sleeping, or see the happiness she felt when she did something for the first time, like the night flight in my plane. Just simple things.

She opened her eyes a few moments later to find me watching her again, but this time she just smiled and looked happy.

"Let's go swimming," I blurted.

"What?"

"A body of water—you and me moving around in it."

"You have a pool? Here?"

"Yeah, I like to swim. I've been having the place renovated slowly and the indoor pool house was done up last year. From the outside it looks like it belongs with the rest of the place, but inside it's very modern. Sort of like this room."

"I wondered about that. I like your bedroom, but I also loved the traditional décor in the room where I stayed last time."

"So, do you think I should preserve everything at Donadea in its original form and design, then?"

She seemed to really think about it for a minute before answering. "Well, I'm all for preserving history, of course, but this is also your home—your sanctuary—and you love being here, so I think you need to make it fit so it's comfortable for you to enjoy when you visit the place."

I kissed her softly. "You just scored some points, Miss Hargreave. I like your answer."

She did a fist pump and mouthed the words, "I scored points."

"You so did. Now, do you want to have a swim with me?"

"I don't have a suit to wear."

"Wear your knickers if you like."

"Will anybody see?"

"Just you and me." I gave her arse a playful smack before hopping out of bed to find some shorts to throw on.

When I came out of my closet her knickers were

back on and she was coming out of the bathroom putting her arms through the straps of her bra, trying to do it up.

"Absolutely not." I snatched that thing out of her hands and tossed it over my shoulder.

She squinted her pretty eyes, sending me what I was sure had to be something along the lines of *What is your problem, you fucking arsehole!* The feisty kitten was ready to hiss at me, and I absolutely loved it.

I palmed both of her breasts, one in each hand, and held them reverently. "Don't ever cover these when we are alone."

Her frown turned soft in an instant, her mouth sliding into a grin. "Why, Mr. Everley, I do believe you are enamored with my breasts."

I gave her a look. "Not even close, my lovely Miss Hargreave."

"No?" She frowned.

"You have the most spectacular set of tits I've ever had the pleasure of viewing in my life. And *enamored* is a ridiculous word to describe my feelings for your tits."

Her mouth went wide in surprise as she laughed at me.

I buried my face in the decadent cleavage I held in my hands. "Enslaved is a much more appropriate word."

She scoffed and pushed my head away. "You're insane."

"Insane over your tits."

"Well, that's really good to know, Mr. Everley." She put her hands on her hips. "I assume the pool house is a distance from this bedroom, and I need to wear something to cover me. I'm basically naked."

My turn to pout.

"They are too perfect to be covered up and I want to look at them."

"You've made that point abundantly clear and I get it. You like breasts—"

"—very partial to yours in particular."

She stonefaced me again. "Are you deaf?" She pointed to her chest. "If you want me to step out of this room with you, then you'd better find me a robe, or a shirt of yours, or a sheet, or *something* to cover up these *spectacular tits* until we arrive at the pool."

"Fine." Well, she did have a point there. Finnegan was around, and Marjorie could show up anywhere at any time. Better not shock the staff with my debauchery on a Sunday morning. I went back into my closet and dug around until I found something that looked promising. It was blue, made of silk and had a belt. It also looked like something Finnegan might wear to bed, but it was indeed a robe. I really had no idea where half of the shit in my house came from, which was why I wanted to go through decade's worth of the accumulated crap systematically.

Hopefully get rid of most of it.

"Will this do?" I showed her.

Her eyes widened. She fingered the fabric and checked the label. "What is with the smoking jackets and this place?"

"Huh?" I asked.

"Smoking jackets. Fancy robes rich men used to wear for lounging and—"

"—smoking I gather?"

She rolled her eyes at my joke and took the thing off its hangar, holding it out to look more closely. "This is definitely vintage, Ivan, and it has to be at least sixty years old. Sharkskin silk out of the fifties if I had to guess. I buy vintage dresses sometimes so I know a little about heirloom clothing, and they don't come with cheap price tags. This looks expensive to me, and probably valuable. I'd hate to damage it. Are you sure?"

"Of course I'm sure. You said you had to have a robe to cover up your spectacular tits from view, and so you shall." I took it from her and held it open for her to slip on. "You may keep it if you like it. I don't even know why it was in my closet. I never wore it."

She slid one arm through and then the other, easing into it carefully as if she wasn't worthy of the damn thing. That really irritated me. I was jealous of a goddamn fucking robe—and she didn't know it yet, but as soon as we got into the pool house, I'd be tearing it off her.

"It really is beautiful," she said as she ran her hands down the front and reached for the belt. "It fits me pretty well, although I don't think it was ever meant to be this long. Definitely sized for a man." She looked down at her toes peeping out from the hem at the floor. The sleeves were a little long too, but overall the whole effect was really fucking sexy. Her nipples had hardened and I could see the perfect outline of her breasts under the thin silk. Knowing she was basically naked underneath that robe, and also what we'd been doing together for the last hours, was a pretty powerful force to fight off.

But I didn't want to fight anything off with her.

I wanted to keep her—something I'd not wanted to do with anybody for a very long time. I understood I needed to be careful with how to proceed with Gabrielle. She was different. Not typical in how she viewed the world, or even in how she behaved within it. Somehow, I knew the things I'd done before to charm women, were not going to work with her. She was also a runner, I'd learned.

She ran away when she was scared.

But this was the heart of my problem, and I needed to figure her out.

"Beautiful. I agree, Miss Hargreave." Again, she had no idea I was referring to her and not the pretentious robe, which was now preventing me from enjoying the view of her spectacular tits.

Gabrielle was that perfectly unspoiled.

I kept my promise and ditched her robe as soon as we got into the pool house. We held hands and jumped in together. She dared me to do it. Competitive Gabrielle was as incredibly sexy as the submissive Gabrielle I'd just had underneath me taking my cock to perfection.

She looked like a water goddess in my pool. Wet hair plastered over her skin and breasts. Hard nipples peeking through enough to tease me. Absolutely no hesitation when I challenged her to a race of four laps. She even gave me some opposition because she was a strong swimmer, but I didn't let her win. I guessed right. She would've been greatly displeased if I had.

She got back at me for the win by mocking me with a glimpse of her arse in those thong knickers, and then topped that off with a huge kick of water to the head.

"That's it, you're done," I said, going down and tugging her underwater with me. She surprised me again by grabbing my face and kissing me before I could even do much more than grab her. I reluctantly brought us up to the surface still kissing, and wondering how she'd turned everything around on me.

I got my hands under her bum and lifted her up. She wrapped her legs around my hips and released my lips, still holding my face in her two hands.

Her green eyes looked very mischievous. "You were saying something about me being *done*, Mr. Everley? Are you sure, because it doesn't feel like it to me." She ground her hips forward and right down on my awakening cock.

Instinct took over and I thrust back, my thoughts instantly going forward with possibilities of where we were going to shag next. Edge of the pool? Chaise lounge? Grotto shower?

God, she was so perfect, and I was so…captivated. I lowered my lips to lick at her wet nipple before closing around it, drawing it in for a full suck. She leaned back to give me more access and gasped a small sound of pleasure. So responsive and lush like this—

The echoing creak of the doors opening got our attention when Finnegan entered with a rolling cart and wearing an apron. Gabrielle squeaked and slid down in the water, arms crisscrossed over her bare breasts. I stepped in front of her to shield her a little more, and gave Finnegan a face full of, *What in the hell are you up to, old man?*

THANK God Ivan stepped in front of me. Mr. Finnegan was here and had to have seen me cavorting naked in the pool with his employer. Mortified much? I couldn't even begin to imagine what he thought of me now, considering my emotional state the last time he'd laid eyes on me.

"Breakfast, my Lord, for you and Miss Hargreave. Welcome back to Donadea, miss."

I peered around Ivan but kept my body under the water. "Hello, Mr. Finnegan. Thank you for the breakfast, and the welcome." God, I wanted to duck completely under and swim away.

He tilted his head at me politely. "Miss Hargreave, you left some of your clothes behind in your room when you departed previously. I've taken the liberty of laundering your things, and have placed them in Mr. Everley's bedroom should you like to…have them back in your possession." He cleared his throat and stood ramrod straight waiting for me to respond.

"Oh." My muddy clothes I'd left on the floor. "Thank you. How sweet of you to do that for me. I figured you would have thrown them out."

I nodded in thanks like an idiot, hovering behind Ivan. Two thoughts came to mind: I now had some clothes to wear which was a good thing, but the evidence I'd just spent the night in bed sexing up the boss, out there for open speculation—not so much. I'm sure my face was the color of a beet. And why was Ivan so silent just standing in the pool saying nothing like a mute? I poked him in the side with my elbow.

I felt him react and peer down at me in question.

I kept my fake smile plastered to my face trained on Mr. Finnegan. Ivan could swing in the breeze for all I cared. This was an every-man-for-himself situation.

"Breakfast, huh? Thank you, Finnegan," he said slowly.

"My pleasure, my Lord. Oh, I nearly forgot to mention, a package arrived a short while ago, addressed to you from Mr. Brinkley. I've delivered that to your bedroom as well."

"Ah, excellent," Ivan answered stiffly.

"Shall I pour?" Mr. Finnegan asked with an outstretched arm toward the cart.

Ivan just stared at him, as if he was trying to make sense of the question, then he glanced down at me again. "Shall Finnegan pour, Gabrielle?"

What? Why are you asking me if Mr. Finnegan shall pour?

"I-I g-guess so if he wants to." Oh. My. God. Did I just say that out loud? This was like a really bad British comedy. Real bad.

I so needed out of this pool and the smoking jacket wrapped around me again.

Ivan grinned down at me, processing my response, and no doubt finding great amusement in my trapped state of naked and wet. He looked like he was trying to suppress some straight-out laughter, but he just turned back and answered Mr. Finnegan easily. "Miss Hargreave says yes."

Mr. Finnegan took that information and proceeded to pour the tea, or coffee, or whatever he'd brought for us.

I shoved Ivan with both of my hands and hissed, "Get out! And bring me a towel so *I* can get out— and the robe, too."

He raised his eyebrows at me.

I kicked him in the shin from under the water. "Hurry, before he finishes pouring!"

Ivan did it for me. He wore that signature cocky smirk on his face the whole time he helped me get out of the pool, dry off with a towel, and still had it while he blocked the view from Mr. Finnegan so I could dress in the robe, but he did do what I asked of him.

"FINNEGAN adores you, you know," Ivan said before putting a forkful of eggs in his mouth.

"What I *know*, is that your statement couldn't be further from the truth."

"He does."

"No, he does not adore me, Ivan. The poor man must think I am the biggest psycho on the planet. You really have no idea what a mess I was that night." I shook my head in disgust. "Just remembering how I was in front of Mr. Finnegan then, horrifies me now, and just again—almost as much."

"You being gracious and very sweet to him is what I just witnessed. He is putty in your hands. And Finnegan doesn't deliver breakfast." He took another bite. "Ever."

"He has always been so kind to me."

"That's because he adores you," he said patiently.

I sipped my tea with milk, made perfectly as if I had prepared it. He must have noticed what I used from the tea cart in the bedroom where I'd slept before. And he had my clothes, too. Mr. Finnegan was my true champion.

"Gabrielle?"

I looked up. Ivan wore a serious expression on his face, telling me he wasn't kidding around at the moment. "Yes?"

"I really do feel like a gormless prick for what happened that night."

I could tell he was being sincere just by the expression of regret in his eyes.

"It's all right. The whole thing was like a Twilight Zone episode. And not all of it was your fault."

He shook his head at me. "I was terribly out of line, and I am so sorry you were frightened and ill while you were here. Finnegan said you were in tears."

"He did?"

"Oh yes. I got the dreaded baronial address from him that morning just like I did a few minutes ago when he brought this breakfast in here."

"What does that mean, baronial address?"

"When he uses *my Lord* on me, Finnegan is undoubtedly telling me to fuck off."

"Wow. That's just crazy," I said in disbelief, wondering what the story was there.

"I hope you forgive me someday."

"It's okay, Ivan. I'm over it. I understand the mistaken identity now, and you should know I was extra fragile that night because I was coming down with strep throat. I am not a weepy girl normally, but I felt so physically ill on top of everything else, I guess I just couldn't cope. Mr. Finnegan definitely saw me at my very worst, times a hundred."

He tilted his head a little, his expression a bit unbelieving, and said, "I'm glad Finnegan was so helpful and kind to you then. At least somebody was."

"He tried to feed me breakfast the next morning. Even tempted me with fresh scones, but I declined in my delirium." I picked up a scone with jam off my plate and took a bite of the decadent treat. "Mmm...I totally should have stayed just for his scones."

He smiled at my comment but his smile looked forced, as if he still felt badly for what had happened with us. So many questions rolled through my mind about Ivan Everley. Why the escorts? Surely he'd have zero problems finding a woman willing to give up some sex. Why was he still single? I'd guess he was in his early thirties, and his wealth was obvious, so why still unattached when he looked the way he did? Smoking hot gorgeous. Even now, I could hardly believe I was here with him enjoying this intimate breakfast in his private indoor pool house that looked like something out of Architectural Digest with its dark wood ceiling, glass tiles and slick lighting, stocked with modern comforts like chaise lounges and grotto showers. Why was he still pursuing me even after discovering I wasn't one of his escorts? Why did he want me back at Donadea so badly? Why was he paranoid about being blackmailed?

"What are you thinking about, Gabrielle?"

I decided to tell him the truth. "I'm thinking about what a mystery you are to me. Why do you hire escorts to be with you? I know now we first met under mistaken identity, that you thought I was Maria-the-escort in my green dress, but now that you know I'm not, why do you want to be with me? And why did you want me here enough to kidnap me from Brynne and Ethan's wedding?"

He never took his eyes off me as he answered my questions one by one. "It's you that I find a mystery, so I suppose we're even there." He tapped his long fingers on the edge of the table. "The escorts are now out of the picture for good, but I used the service because I—I don't have a great deal of trust in my past relationships with…women, I suppose. The women I've known all had a purpose in being with me, or merely wanted something from me…but not necessarily *me*, if that makes any sense." He reached across the table and tapped the top of my hand with his index finger. "Now *you*, Miss Hargreave, have been an obsession since our first meeting, it's true. But you keep running away from me for some reason and I need to put a definite stop to that." He sent me a friendly wink. "I contacted the service the day after the Mallerton Gala and arranged another date with *Maria,* and was devastated when you didn't show up. Honest to God truth." He caught me with the intensity in his deep green eyes and gave me a really beautiful smile, the gap between his front teeth making him appear very sincere and real to me right now. He picked up my hand in his and intertwined our fingers. "And I kidnapped you last night and brought you here, because when fate dropped you right back into my lap after two month's wait, after I'd given up hope of ever finding you again, I decided not to be a fucking moron and waste my golden opportunity."

Wow. Not at all what I expected him to tell me.

At all.

He was devastated when I didn't show up as Maria?

His answers were a little much for me to accept, but it was hard not feel the sincerity from him.

"But why me and not somebody who runs in your circles?"

"Because nobody that runs in my circles, as you put it, has made me feel this good in a very long time, Gabrielle."

I had to look down at my plate. It was still difficult to take in what he was telling me, but I did believe him. Ivan had a way of presenting himself as truthful, or it sure felt like it to me.

Because nobody has made me feel this good in a very long time, Gabrielle. For whatever reasons, I made him feel good. Did he even know how good being with him made me feel?

"Look at me." He spoke the words firmly, but not in a harsh way. Just as meaningful and compelling as he'd spoken to me from the very beginning.

I did.

I looked up at Ivan in all his glory: long hair wet from the pool and scraped back by his fingers combing through it; golden bare chest dotted with a few lingering drops of water; tattoo of what looked like the zodiac symbol for Sagittarius on his left shoulder, only revealed as he sat relaxed on a towel across the table from me.

He hadn't let go of my hand either.

Devastatingly attractive, and deadly to my will to remain aloof and unaffected by him. I don't think it was possible for me to be unaffected.

There was far too much gorgeousness blessed upon Ivan Everley for one human man to own, but very blessed he had been.

And if he didn't watch out he would make me fall for him, with his soulful words and seductively commanding ways. If it wasn't too late for me already.

"I've never brought a woman here before in the way you're here with me right now." His eyes held onto me. "You are the first, Gabrielle Hargreave. And furthermore, I think you should stay and do the job of cataloging my ridiculously large collection of paintings." He picked up my hand and brought it up to his lips still entangled in his own. "I want you here. Very much."

Damn, he is good.

His expression was one of adoration, respect, desire. I wanted to stay with him. I wanted to be the object of his desire.

Priceless

Perhaps it was already too late for me.
Perhaps I was already falling.

Chapter 14

I could see the struggle going on in her mind as clearly as if she'd just told me her inner thoughts. It reminded me a little of a competition. The moment when you know you've gotten into your opponent's head. It was like that with Gabrielle right now. All I had to do was stay in her head, and convince her she wanted the same thing as me.

"No worries. I still have plenty of time to work on you. The day is young."

Her face fell, and then changed to panic.

"Ivan, what time is it?"

"It's early. Probably not more than half past ten."

"Oh shit. The morning-after wedding brunch is today at noon. We are supposed to be there, Ivan, both of us. And we're—we are in Ireland right now!" she hissed, throwing down her napkin and jumping up from the table. "I have to get showered and dressed—and—and then you have to fly me back to Hallborough."

She turned away from me and ran toward the shower grotto.

Well, fuck. It looked like there was still some convincing to do with my beautiful obsession. And I remembered what I already knew about her. She was a runner whenever something frightened her.

The only thing to do with a runner is to run even faster so you can catch them.

SHE was already washing her hair when I came up behind her in the pool house showers. I watched her for a moment as she hurried to do everything in a rush. I needed to slow her down.

"Gabrielle."

She turned and dunked her head under the spray

and let the shampoo rinse out of her long dark hair, her eyes closed tightly, not acknowledging me.

I pulled her against my chest, my hands linked behind her back so she couldn't push away. Her breasts pressed into my chest, soft and wet as I put my lips to hers.

Her hands came up to my chin and faltered. Maybe in defense—or possibly just protecting herself from me—but it was still an acceptance, and she didn't do more than just hold her trembling hands suspended between us while I kissed her under the shower spray.

I could work with that.

A kiss was intimate, and helped me to dig my way further under her skin.

I know how to win, using every small thing to my advantage in order to get there. I had the medals to prove it.

She was my win. My gold medal.

Winning Gabrielle would be my toughest competition yet.

But so worth it. So fucking worth it in the end.

I kept her against me under the shower for another moment, slowing everything down with her, taking the panic out of the moment.

I brought my hands up to cup her cheeks, holding and directing the angle of her head until all of the shampoo was rinsed away. I turned off the water and kept her face in my hands. The shower head drained out its last drops, falling onto the tile floor in a steady rhythm at our feet.

She cast her eyes up at me, so unsure and fearful. I could see the fear in every flicker of their lovely hue. Her eyes were a unique shade of green, flecked with other variants of colours from brown to yellow to blue.

"The rest of the weekend, Gabrielle. Give that to me."

She shook her head still held in my two hands. "No. I have to go back. You said you'd take me—."

"—even if we took off this very minute we can't make it back to Hallborough by noon. It's impossible."

"But we won't be there for the brunch then," she whispered, defeated.

I rubbed my thumbs over the sides of her jaw. "Think about it. People won't be looking for us. They'll be waiting on the bride and groom, and while Ethan and Brynne might notice we're absent, I'm sure they'll be more anxious to get away on their honeymoon. They won't care."

"Maybe...," she said biting on one side of her luscious bottom lip. "But Ben will wonder where I am, and Elaina will, too. They will ask around for me."

"I'm sure Fred has noticed my plane is gone from his lake by now. I can message Hannah and say I brought you over to Donadea for a quick visit so you could get a glimpse of my paintings. It's mostly the truth." I smiled at her. "I just leave out the part about kidnapping you when you were under the influence of one too many blueberry mojitos, and they'll be none the wiser."

"I don't even have my purse or my phone with me, Ivan. I'm sure that doesn't look too smooth if anyone figures it out."

"If you know his number, you can call your friend and speak to him in person, so he won't worry about you. Explain to him how my offer of so many priceless works of art was more than you could resist. That you were impulsive after a few drinks and dancing."

"But all of my clothes and my phone...we just left there with nothing."

"Tell him I'm having your things delivered to Donadea from Hallborough and will take you directly to London when we have to go back."

"You will?"

"Of course. I left my things there as well, and I'll speak with Hannah and ask her to pack it up for us. She'll do it no question. She is the absolute best, and she knows how to keep silent. You'll have no gossip worries coming from my cousin."

I could tell her cogs were spinning, puzzling out my suggestions and on the verge of agreeing, so I pushed her a little bit more.

"Is there anything back at Hallborough you'd rather have than this?"

I didn't give her chance to answer my question, though. I just lowered my head and backed up enough to get my mouth over one of her tits, and started sucking.

She settled exactly into the pull and push of my lips and tongue, letting me go to work on her, entrusting her pleasure to me.

I loved how she melted in my arms when I touched her, became soft and wanton. It drove me to madness, to a point where I didn't ponder much at all beyond making her come again.

Giving an orgasm to Gabrielle had become my new favorite fucking job.

I asked her again. "Is there anything back there you'd rather be doing, Gabrielle?"

I slid my fingers under the lace of her knickers and impaled two of them up into her soaked pussy.

"Nooooo," she cried on a shuddering moan, her knees buckling a bit as I starting stroking my fingers in and out of her tight heat.

"Good gorgeous girl," I said, winding her tighter and tighter with each slide of my fingers matched against the sucking pulls of my mouth on her tits. I had her pinned up against the shower wall, quivering and shaking under me as I sorted her out, taking from her what I demanded she give up. I knew I couldn't stop, nor would I stop, until she was blissfully pleasured and drooping in my arms.

Then, and only then, I'd carry her back up to my bedroom and fuck us both to sleep. Wake up after a while and maybe fuck some more if we wanted to. Lowell had seen to the condoms being delivered as I'd asked. I had everything I needed to convince Gabrielle to stay with me a bit longer.

And convince her I would.

SO I went from living in a sexual desert to a banging rainforest of jungle-love in the matter of about twelve hours. How in the hell did that happen? *Ivan happened, that's how.*

After the shower *conversation* with Ivan, I don't remember much except being carried up the big stairs at some point. I'd been utterly lost to the sensation of total erotic bliss at his hands, and mouth, and his cock that I didn't really care about the particulars. It all felt too damn good.

He was an amazing lover.

Ben was going to be relentless grilling me about what I'd been doing with Ivan. Ben! "Shit, I never phoned Benny!" I leaped out of bed, grabbing the first thing I could put in my hand around. The vintage smoking jacket. The elegance of the thing made me feel like a rich man's mistress from an old black and white movie, which was kind of true, and strange both at the same time.

Ivan cocked open an eye and surveyed me from head to toe, completely at ease with his own lack of coverings, totally nude with his arm stretched out toward me, seemingly unconcerned by my current panic. He must be used to them by now. It wasn't the first since we been spending time together.

"He's probably left me fifty messages and texts by now—"

"—Gabrielle."

"—and Filan, my God, she's likely to be right in the thick of the speculation—"

"—Gabrielle! I phoned Hannah earlier while you were sleeping." His voice had an edge to it which commanded respect, silencing my panicked rant immediately.

"You did?"

He nodded slowly. "Talked to her and explained everything about packing up our things and also asked her to let Clarkson know where you are. All taken care of. We might even have everything delivered by morning. My assistant will get it all organized for us straight away."

I sat on the edge of the bed and tried to process all that Ivan had done so we could have this weekend together. "You must *really* want me to stay here, if you went to all that trouble," I said quietly.

"It was no trouble, and yes, I really want you here."

I studied him boldly, admiring his body for the beautiful specimen it truly was. I thought about all the ways he'd been using it on me, too. Sex, just for the enjoyment of the experience with another like-minded person, was pretty amazing, but I'd be fooling myself if I couldn't admit I was enjoying other aspects besides the sex and the orgasms. I liked the attention he paid to me—and the physical contact, the touches—and the way he kissed me, too. Ivan liked to kiss. And I'd decided I really liked kissing Ivan.

"I wish you believed me," he said.

"I am trying to understand why me?"

He sighed and gave me a patient look. "If you'll take that goddamn robe off and crawl over here I can work on some more explanations of precisely 'why you.'"

"More?" It didn't escape my notice that his cock had lengthened and was growing thick again.

"I'm a dedicated fellow determined to fully convince you." He gave me a slow grin that just travelled up on one side of his sexy mouth.

I stood up and slowly untied the belt of my adopted robe, removing it carefully one little bit at a time. I liked the look of him while he watched me. He made me feel very sensual and special.

So when I crawled over to him, and he showed me, yet again, how good he could make us both feel, I let him do it. I let Ivan take me to another place in my body and mind because it felt too wonderful for me to deny.

GABRIELLE knew how to suck cock. Well, she was spectacularly good at sucking mine. I didn't like to think about how she'd learnt her skills, but I'd have to overlook that part if I wanted to keep her.

And I did want to keep her.

I knew it now. There had been hints as we'd begun this tryst, but now, I knew for certain that my dream girl did, in fact, exist. And she was naked in my arms after a supremely satisfying session of her mouth on my cock, an experience I couldn't compare to anything similar I'd ever received in my life. She enjoyed doing it, too.

After sex, she tended to be quiet, just content to let me kiss her and stroke my fingers over her flushed skin, so it surprised me when she hit me with words I didn't want to hear.

"Ivan…I don't think it's a good idea for you to employ me now that we've—because we have been together intimately—it's not professional conduct—I really can't." She faltered and then trailed off, the disappointing silence rising between us.

My sexy kitten wasn't going to be easy on me it seemed.

"But, just think for a second. Have you done anything with me so far that you didn't enjoy, or didn't give us both a great deal of pleasure?"

"No."

"And you are a qualified conservator of paintings certified through the University of London, yes?"

"You know I am, Ivan."

"So tell me what I have a houseful of, Gabrielle, just moldering away into dust. Tell me, lovely thing, I want to hear you say it."

She shook her head at me in frustration, but I wasn't having it.

"No, Miss Hargreave, I want to hear *you* tell me."

She held onto my eyes, and I knew I'd won this small battle when her shoulders relaxed and she gave into the desires that were very hard to deny. I understood how it worked for her, as well as for me.

"You have so many paintings."

I took her hand and kissed it, holding it pressed to my lips. "I have so many paintings, Gabrielle. And I only want you to have a look at them. Nobody else will do."

"But, it's so unprofessional." She was struggling with something that went beyond just having a sexual relationship with me while working here. There was more to her story I desperately wanted to know. I wanted to know her story just as much as I didn't want her to learn about the sordidness of mine. She was so unspoiled, and knew nothing much about my life, or my past. It was part of the magical allure Gabrielle held over me.

"Does the part about being unprofessional really matter? So we met each other under unusual circumstances. Yes, agreed. But now, we have discovered we like doing this, too." I swept my hand down her body in a caress, coming to rest on the flesh of her arse. "This is a private job anyway. Therefore nobody gets to know what we do together in *private*. It's just between you and me."

She let me kiss her, slowly and thoroughly. My tongue had a way of getting lost inside her anyway, and kissing her soothed me. When I was finally able to pull away, she had her hands buried in my hair again. I guess she had a thing for touching my hair, and I thought it was fucking hot. She could bury her hands in my hair when I was buried in her, as much and as often as she liked.

I took her face with both hands and held her still. "I knew I had to get you back here somehow to show you that you were meant to come to Donadea. This place, the paintings hidden away here waiting— was fate for someone like you. I was determined, even after you left here the first time, I would find you and convince you to give me another try."

"You were?" She seemed so surprised.

"Oh yes, my lovely Miss Hargreave."

She offered her lips up to mine for a kiss, which thrilled me to accept from her. She was so sweet and generous. Her offer gave me the courage to tell her the rest of my plan. Because I was going to *tell* her. Telling and directing were actions devoted to my part in this. Her role would be different.

"And Gabrielle, having you archive my paintings and enjoy each other in bed is not the only thing I am proposing here with you."

"What else are you proposing?" she asked

carefully, the slight widening of her eyes a clue as to her own perceptiveness of what was really going on between us, and maybe even what I was going to say next.

"I want you submissive when we fuck, Gabrielle. I want so badly to have that...with you."

THE END
BOOK I

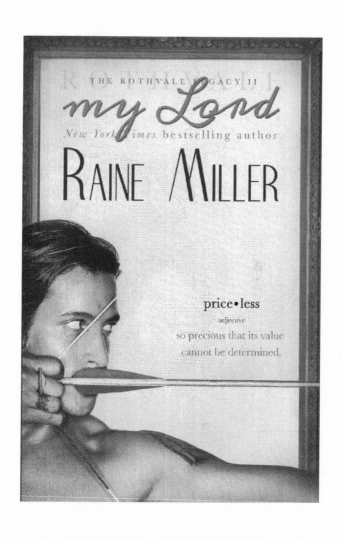

THE ROTHVALE LEGACY II

my Lord

New York Times bestselling author

RAINE MILLER

price•less
adjective
so precious that its value
cannot be determined.

Book II ~ October 2014

If you enjoyed **PRICELESS**, *please consider leaving a review.*

Thank you for reading!

♥

For updates on releases and series sign up for my

Newsletter:

www.rainemiller.com/newsletter/

KIWI BLUEBERRY MOJITOS

Yes, Gabrielle's drink of choice does indeed exist.

And they are gorgeous!

Courtesy of **www.Laylita.com**

Priceless

INGREDIENTS

- 6 kiwis, peeled and cut in half or quartered
- 4 kiwis, peeled and sliced - to be used as garnishes
- 6 ounces of blueberries, to be crushed
- 6 ounce of blueberries, to be kept whole as garnishes
- ¼ cup fresh lime juice, from 1-2 limes
- ~ ½ cup sugar, adjust to taste
- 4 ounce pack of mint, leaves only
- 1 ½ - 2 cups of sparkling water
- 1 to 1 ½ cups of rum, adjust based on your preference
- Ice as needed
- Blue / green sugar to decorate glass rims

INSTRUCTIONS

1. Place the cut kiwis in a small food processor with the sugar and lime juice, pulse until you have coarse puree. Mix the kiwi puree with the rum, you can start by adding the lower amount and then adjust as you prepare the drink.

2. Gently crush the first 6 ounces of blueberries using a muddler.

3. You can make the mojitos in pitcher or in individual glasses.

4. Moisten the rims of the glasses with a slice of lime and garnish the rims with the sugar. If you can't find blue and/or green sugar, you can use blue/green cookie sugar sprinkles.

5. To make it in a pitcher, pour the kiwi puree into the pitcher, add a layer of ice, add a good amount of mint leaves and kiwi slices. Next add a few more ice cubes, and then add the crushed blueberries, some more mint leaves and whole blueberries. Top off with the sparkling water and mix gently. Taste and add more rum, sparkling water, or sugar if needed.

6. To make the drink in individual glasses, follow a similar process as for the pitcher, but add a few whole blueberries at the beginning. You can also add a slice of kiwi with the blueberries at the end.

NOTES

To make this as a *mocktail* variation, just leave out the rum and replace it with additional sparkling water or sparkling lemonade.

ABOUT THE AUTHOR

Raine has been reading romance novels since she picked up that first Barbara Cartland paperback at the tender age of thirteen. She thinks it was *The Flame is Love* from 1975. And it's a safe bet she'll never stop reading romance novels because now she writes them too. Granted, Raine's stories are edgy enough to turn Ms. Cartland in her grave, but to her way of thinking, a tall, dark and handsome hero never goes out of fashion. Never! A former teacher turned full-time writer of sexy romance stories, is how she fills her days. Raine has a prince of a husband, and two brilliant sons to pull her back into the real world if the writing takes her too far away. Her sons know she likes to write stories, but have never asked to read any. (Thank God) She loves to hear from readers and chat about the characters in her books. You can connect with Raine on Facebook at the **Blackstone Affair Fan Page** or visit **www.RaineMiller.com** to sign up for newsletter updates and see what she's working on now.

BOOKS BY RAINE MILLER

The Blackstone Affair

NAKED, Book 1

ALL IN, Book 2

EYES WIDE OPEN, Book 3

RARE and PRECIOUS THINGS, Book 4

♥

CHERRY GIRL, Neil & Elaina I

MY CAPTAIN, Neil & Elaina II

Historical Prequels to The Blackstone Affair

The PASSION of DARIUS

The UNDOING of a LIBERTINE

The MAKING of LADY PERCIVAL

The Rothvale Legacy

PRICELESS, Book I

MY LORD, Book II

Historical Prequels to The Rothvale Legacy

The MUSE

Priceless

NOTES